# THE INVESTIGATION

By the same author in English translation

*Grey Souls* (2005)
*Brodeck's Report* (2009)
*Monsieur Linh and His Child* (2011)

# PHILIPPE CLAUDEL

# THE INVESTIGATION

*Translated from the French by*
*Daniel Hahn*

MACLEHOSE PRESS
QUERCUS · LONDON

First published in the French language as L'Enquête
by Éditions Stock, Paris, in 2010
First published in Great Britain in 2013 by

MacLehose Press
an imprint of Quercus
55 Baker Street
7th Floor, South Block
London W1U 8EW

This book is supported by the Institut Français
as part of the Burgess programme.
(www.frenchbooknews.com)

INSTITUT
FRANÇAIS

A CIP catalogue record for this book is available
from the British Library.

ISBN (HB) 978 0 85705 154 7
ISBN (TPB) 978 0 85705 155 4
ISBN (Ebook) 978 0 85705 156 1

For those who come after,
so that they are not the next

"Seek nothing. Forget"
*Hell*, Henri-Georges Clouzot

# 1

AS HE STEPPED OUT OF THE STATION THE INVESTIGATOR WAS met by a fine rain mingled with wet, slushy snow. He was a small man, roundish, without much hair. Everything about him was commonplace, from his clothes to the expression on his face, and if someone had been asked to describe him, in the setting of a novel, for example, or of criminal proceedings or a legal deposition, he would certainly have had quite some trouble creating a detailed portrait. He was, in a way, a fading being, no sooner seen than forgotten. He was as insubstantial as the fog, as dreams, or as a breath exhaled by a mouth and, as such, he was just like billions of other human beings.

The station square was identical to countless station squares, with its distribution of impersonal buildings all pressed against one another. Running along the top of one of them, an advertising billboard bore the photograph, disproportionately enlarged, of an old man who fixed on whoever looked at him, an amused, melancholy gaze. It was impossible to read the slogan that accompanied the photograph – perhaps it did not even have one? – as the top of the billboard was lost in the clouds.

The sky crumbled and fell in a sodden dust that melted on shoulders and seeped right into bodies without being invited. It was not really cold, but the dampness acted like an octopus whose thin tentacles managed to find their way into the tiniest gaps between clothes and skin.

The Investigator was there, quite still, for a quarter of an hour, standing very straight, his suitcase on the ground beside him, as the raindrops and the snowflakes continued to die on his head and his raincoat. He did not move. Not even a little. And for this long moment, he thought of nothing.

No car passed. No pedestrian. They had forgotten him. It was not the first time. Finally he turned up the collar of his raincoat, gripped the handle of his suitcase and decided – before he got utterly soaked – to cross the square and go into a bar that already had its lights on, even though a clock attached to a street lamp a few metres away from him was showing not even four in the afternoon.

The room was strangely deserted and the Barman, who was half-asleep behind the counter, distractedly following the results of the horse racing on a television screen, threw him a somewhat unfriendly glance, then, while the Investigator had already had time to remove his raincoat, to sit down and wait a little, asked him glumly:

"What'll it be?"

The Investigator was not very thirsty, or very hungry. He just needed somewhere to sit before getting himself where he was meant to be. To sit and run through it all. Prepare what he was going to say. In a sense to make a gradual entry into his character as Investigator.

"A grog," he said at last.

But the Barman replied immediately:

"I'm sorry, that won't be possible."

"You don't know how to make a grog?" the Investigator asked, surprised.

The Barman shrugged.

"Of course I do, but that drink doesn't appear in our computer listing, and the automated till would refuse to register a charge for it."

The Investigator almost said something, but restrained himself, sighed, and ordered a sparkling water.

Outside the rain had yielded to the relentless progress of the snow, which was now falling, light and swirling, almost unreal, in a slow-motion movement that seemed to be deliberately controlling its effects. The Investigator watched the flakes raise up a folding screen before him. It was scarcely possible to make out the façade of the station, and not at all possible to see the platforms in the distance, the tracks, the waiting trains. It was as though someone had erased the place where he had stopped a little earlier to step into this new world, a world at the heart of which he now had to get his bearings.

"Winter today," the Barman said, putting a small bottle of water he had just uncapped down on the table. He was not looking at the Investigator, but at the snowflakes. In fact, he had spoken these words without even addressing them to him, as though the thought had just escaped from his brain to flutter a bit around his skull, like a poor insect resigned to the knowledge that it was doomed to disappear at any moment, but who despite everything is determined to keep the show going, to play its part as an insect right up to the very end, even if this interests no-one and will not save it from anything.

And the Barman stayed like that, standing beside the table, still, quite ignoring the Investigator, for a long while, his gaze hypnotised by the snow, which, beyond the glass, rushed its milky particles in trajectories that were elegant but entirely without logic.

## 2

THE INVESTIGATOR COULD HAVE SWORN HE HAD SEEN TWO OR three taxis when he came out of the station. Taxis waiting with their engines running, their headlamps on, their exhaust fumes grey and delicate and dissolving as soon as they leaked into the air. The taxis must have gone off somewhere, with their customers sitting warm in the back seats. It was too tiresome.

The snow had decided to linger a little. It was still falling, imposing its presence like a monarch. The Investigator had asked the Barman for directions. He had expected an unfriendly reply, but the man had seemed happy to supply him with the information: it wasn't all that difficult, to tell the truth, The Firm was enormous, he couldn't miss it. It spilled out everywhere. Whichever road he took, he couldn't help running into a surrounding wall, a screen door, an access route, a warehouse, a loading dock belonging to The Firm.

"One way or another," the Barman had added, "*everything* here more or less belongs to The Firm." He had emphasised the everything.

"And then," he had gone on, "all you have to do is follow the outer wall round till you get to the main entrance and the Guard-house."

Then he had gone back to his horse race. His eyes glued to the television screen with thoroughbreds a-lather galloping across it, his elbows resting on the bar, his head in his hands, the Barman had not reacted when the Investigator said goodbye, passing through the front door to walk out of his life.

In any case, his function had come to an end there.

It was not quite night yet, but there was still a very real nocturnal atmosphere, increased by the utter solitude in which the Investigator moved, walking along the snow-covered pavements, never meeting a living soul, only occasionally having any sense that he was actually passing through an inhabited world when his little silhouette entered the circle of creamy yellow light from a street lamp, and remained there for a few metres before moving back into the thick, unfathomable regions of dusk.

The suitcase was getting heavier. His raincoat was sopping wet. The Investigator went on, without thinking. He was shivering more and more. His thoughts wandered as aimlessly as his icy, painful feet. All of a sudden he pictured himself as a convict, as an outlaw, as the last man alive, as a survivor searching for a refuge after having fled some final chemical, ecological or nuclear disaster. He felt his own body becoming his enemy, and walked in a dream. It went on and on. He had the impression that he had been wandering for hours. All the streets were identical. The snow erased every point of reference in its abstract uniformity. Was he going round in circles?

The collision had been soundless and momentary. Yet this had not prevented it from dazing him badly. He had crashed into a man, or a woman, he wasn't too sure, in any case some human form, hurtling through the night, against him, at a moderate pace but unstoppable. Apologies, a few polite words on his part. From the other person, nothing, only mutterings, the sound of the footsteps moving away. The night dissolving a silhouette.

Still a dream?

No, something had remained from the incident: a sharp pain in his left shoulder and on his forehead, which he was rubbing, and onto which the dying flakes dripped. And then, of course, there was the suitcase. The suitcase. Scattered across the ground, exploded, calling to mind all those pieces of luggage seen in news reports, floating on the sea after countless air crashes, the final witnesses of lives that have been jostled by the currents, lives that have disappeared, been pulverised, reduced to nothingness, to sweaters heavy with salt water, trousers that are still moving even though they no longer contain a single leg, cuddly toys shocked to discover that the arms of the children who clung to them have been lost for ever.

The Investigator struggled to gather back up the five shirts, the underwear, the pyjamas, the toiletries, and he crushed the tube of toothpaste under the sole of his shoe and it spread onto the ground like a large pink and blue worm smelling of artificial mint, the terylene trousers, the alarm clock, the pairs of socks, the laundry bag, still empty, the electric razor and its unruly cable. Finally he closed the suitcase again, which was now a little heavier, because besides all his belongings, it was now carrying an extra weight of snow, and rain, and melancholy.

But he really ought to keep on walking, through the night, proper night time now, finding this deserted town increasingly inhospitable – deserted but for those shadows with compact bodies like a bull's, capable of throwing a man off course with a single clump from its horns. And to cap it all, he started to sneeze, three times, violently. There was no doubt about it, tomorrow morning he would wake up with his nose running, his throat dry and rough, tight as a vice, his feverish head ringed by a barrel on which someone was banging again and again. Those early hours of the morning were going to be a real horror. Oh, waking up like that, he said to himself, and then having to begin a long and undoubtedly tedious day of investigation – just my luck!

Yes, waking up. In a bedroom, to be sure. But in what bedroom?

# 3

SO THAT WAS THE GUARDROOM? BUT IT DID NOT LOOK ANYTHING like a guardroom, and what surrounded it looked nothing like the entrance to a firm, still less to The Firm.

The Investigator had passed to and fro this place three or four times, never suspecting that it could be the Guardroom: a sort of blockhouse, a massive rhomboid of unfinished concrete, interspersed at irregular intervals by narrow vertical openings, as thin as arrow-slits. The whole thing gave off an impression of absolute closure. This building defined anyone approaching it as an intruder, an enemy even. The chevaux-de-frise set out here and there suggested the imminent threat of attacks that had to be fended off, and the rolls of barbed wire, the portcullises, the chicanes it was possible to make out beyond them reinforced this sense of a potential menace. Images sprang to the Investigator's mind of fortified embassies in countries at war. But The Firm was not an embassy, and the country was not at war. Beyond that outer wall the only things being produced – according to his briefing – were harmless pieces of communications equipment, and the software for operating them, pieces with no strategic value, and whose production had not been the object of any real secrecy for quite some time. There was really nothing to justify this military set-up.

Eventually the Investigator found an enquiry window in the side of the building, as well as a bell set into the outside of the wall. On the other side of the thick glass – bullet-proof glass? – behind the window, a surgical light illuminated a room a few metres square. It was possible to make out a desk, a chair, a calendar pinned to the wall as well as a large panel with dozens of little light bulbs in rows, some of them lit up, others unlit, others blinking. On the left-hand wall, the monitors made up a regular mosaic that offered views of The Firm: offices, warehouses, car parks, staircases, deserted work-shops, cellars, loading bays.

The snow had stopped falling. The Investigator was shivering. He could no longer feel his nose. He had turned up the collar of his raincoat as much as he could to protect his neck, but it was absolutely soaked now and this did nothing but multiply his discomfort. He pressed the bell. Nothing happened. He pressed again. He waited. He glanced around him, called out without much hope as there was no human sound to be heard. Only mechan-ical noises, the purring of engines, or of boilers, or electrical generators, mingled with the murmur of the wind as it gained in strength.

"What is it?"

The Investigator jumped. The words – crackling and rather aggressive – had come from the mouth of an intercom just to the left of the bell.

"Hello," the Investigator managed to say once he had got over his surprise.

"Good evening," returned the voice, which seemed to be coming from very far away, from the depths of a hellish world. The Investigator apologised, explained his presence, said who he was, recounted his arrival at the station, the café, the instructions from the Barman, his wandering hither and thither, the wrong directions he had taken, his walking one way and then the other in front of the . . . The voice interrupted him right in the middle of a sentence.

"Do you hold Exceptional Authorisation?"

"I beg your pardon? I don't understand."

"Do you hold Exceptional Authorisation?"

"Exceptional Auth—? I'm the Investigator . . . I don't know what you're talking about. My arrival was certainly anticipated. I was expected . . ."

"For the last time, have you got Exceptional Authorisation, yes or no?"

"No, but I'm sure I'll have it tomorrow," faltered the Investigator, who was gradually beginning to go to pieces, "when I'm able to find a Person In Charge."

"Without Exceptional Authorisation you are not authorised to breach the outer wall of The Firm after nine p.m."

The Investigator was about to retort that it was only . . . but he glanced at his watch and said nothing: it was almost a quarter to ten. How was that possible? So he had been walking for hours? How could he have lost track of time like that?

"Oh, I'm sorry, I hadn't realised it was so late."

"Come back tomorrow."

He heard what sounded like a cleaver coming down onto a butcher's block. The crackling stopped. He began to shiver even more. His shoes, which were too thin for the season, were filled with water. The ends of his trousers had begun to resemble a floor-cloth. His fingers were going numb. He pressed the bell again.

"What now?" came the distant voice, which was furious this time.

"I do apologise for troubling you again, but I don't know where to sleep."

"We are not a hotel."

"Indeed not – could you possibly point me in the direction of one?"

"We are not the Tourist Office."

The voice disappeared. This time the Investigator understood that it would be useless to ring again. He was overcome by a great weariness, while at the same time panic was making his heart beat at an unaccustomed pace. He brought his hand to his chest. Through the layers of wet clothing he felt the hurried rhythm, the organ's muffled blows against the wall of flesh. It was as though someone were knocking at a door, an inside door, in desperation, a door that was firmly shut, with no-one willing to answer or open it up.

# 4

THE SITUATION WAS BECOMING LUDICROUS. HE HAD NEVER KNOWN a strange misadventure like it. He even rubbed his eyes, bit his lips, to convince himself that everything that had happened to him in the last few hours had not simply been a nightmare.

But no, he really was there, standing at the entrance that was not any kind of entrance, in front of the wall of The Firm that was nothing like any other firm, right beside a guardroom quite different from a normal guardroom, his teeth chattering, sopping wet to his marrow, past ten o'clock at night, while – doubtless to heighten his stupor still further – the rain had regained the upper hand over the snow and was now hammering on his skull.

He was dragging his suitcase more than carrying it. Its contents were no longer clothes but stones, cast iron, steel girders, hunks of granite. Each step he took was accompanied by a shushing noise, like the sound of a sponge being squeezed. The pavements were becoming great swamps. He would not have been any more surprised if his body had been dragged at any moment down into the bottomless depths of a puddle. But suddenly he remembered –

and this restored some feeling of hope – that over the course of his odyssey he had spotted down one of the streets to his right, he remembered that it was on his right, but what good would that direction do him, he had spotted a lit-up sign, and he believed, though at that point he left the realm of certainties, he would not have been ready to stake his life on it, that it was the sign for a hotel. Hotels – there were definitely some on the outskirts of the Town, on its noisy fringes where the motorway interchanges carried out their functions and purged the freeways of any excess stream of cars, operating crucial bloodlettings, separating lives and destinies. But there was no question – on foot, in weather like this – of undertaking such a journey as to reach them. And in any case, which way to go? He knew precisely nothing.

And to think that a simple action could have spared him all this trouble: if he had thought to recharge his telephone before leaving his apartment that morning, he'd be asleep by now in a nice warm bed, listening to the rain drumming on the roof of the hotel he'd have found without the slightest trouble by calling an information number. But the small, inert, useless object that occasionally he felt in his raincoat pocket whenever he passed the suitcase from his left hand to his right, or vice versa, reminded him of his carelessness and his stupidity.

What could the time be? He did not dare look at his watch. He was worn out, chilled to the bone. He sneezed every few metres and his nose was running like a warm tap, malfunctioning and half-closed. And yet wasn't he going to end up being forced to sleep in the train station, on a bench, like so many homeless people? But then he remembered that in this country the train stations had begun to chain up their doors at night precisely to prevent them being transformed into dormitories, and that, moreover, public benches had for years been designed in such a way as to prevent people from stretching out on them.

He proceeded at random, no longer recognising anything. He went past junctions, along the side of buildings, crossed areas filled with detached houses with unlit windows, as if nobody in this town was up at night. No vehicle travelled the streets. Not a car. Not a motorcycle. Not a bicycle. Nothing. It was as if a sort of curfew had imposed a ban on any kind of movement on the territory of the Town.

The Barman had not been lying: The Firm was always there. Near or far, he could make out the dark conglomeration of its facilities, which, behind the icy streaks of rain, took the form of ramparts, high walls that were sometimes crenellated and always thick and suffocating. And then there was its murmur, in spite of the sound of the drops of water on the pavement, a perceptible sound, constant, low, that reminded him of the noise of a refrigerator whose door has been left open.

The Investigator felt old and discouraged, even though his investigation had not even begun, even though as yet nothing had really begun. The rain intensified in strength, just like the wind that swept systematically through the streets, dousing them in a kind of breath – earthy, fetid, glacial – that eventually numbed him.

He had been walking for . . . for how long, actually? He no longer knew, as he walked in a section without a single building to be seen. The pavements were lined with a concrete barrier about three metres high on the crest of which glistened countless shards of glass set in the cement, and the narrow streets, which continued endlessly to branch out from one another, reinforced his unpleasant sense of having become a kind of rodent caught in an outsized trap. The monotonous, oppressive landscape had finally disoriented him, and as he went on he had the peculiar sensation of being watched by some invisible creature, situated somewhere very high above him, mocking his pitiable misfortune.

# 5

AT FIRST HE TOLD HIMSELF THAT EXHAUSTION WAS MAKING HIM
see mirages. And then the name on the unlit sign – "Hotel Hope" –
this had brought him some comfort, too, with the thought that
someone (a sort of game-master) was watching his reaction with a
subtle smile and was playing a good joke on him. He almost wept
with joy, but settled for laughing – lengthy bursts of laughter.
Admittedly, the sign was unlit (and in any case, was this the same
one he had thought he'd seen illuminated some hours earlier?) but
it truly was a hotel, a real hotel, a modest one, undoubtedly rather
antiquated to judge from its shabby façade and its peeling shutters,
some of which were held only by a single hinge, but a hotel that
was in operation according to the notice indicating the rating of
the establishment (four stars! – though one would have been hard
put, on the basis of its façade, to assign it even one at best), the
prohibitive room rates, as well as the cleanliness of the entrance hall
he could see through the glass door, and also the tiny lamp that
gave off a Lilliputian glow over a sort of counter to the left of which
it was possible to make out dozens of mismatching keys hanging
from butcher's hooks.

The Investigator, who had practically run across the road, somewhat breathless, tried in vain for several minutes to find the night bell: there was none. But he was still quite sure that his ordeal had come to an end, and he did not care about the cost. He was prepared to shell out a fortune to get himself into the dry, into the warmth, to stretch out in a bed. Tomorrow there would be time to seek out a hotel more in keeping with his means.

He gave the door a few discreet knocks and waited. Nothing happened. He knocked again, a little harder, thinking that the Night Watchman really couldn't be as watchful as all that, imagining him in a deep, comatose sleep. Was it possible that there was no-one here? He shivered and began to shout and bang against the door in a violent burst of energy. Hotel Hope remained hopelessly shut and silent. With the heaviness of a sandbag, the Investigator allowed himself to slide down the door and collapsed onto his suitcase, which he clung on to as though it were someone much loved, or a lifebuoy, in truth an odd sort of lifebuoy, wetter even than the tides it was supposed to save him from.

"What do you want?"

He gave a start and looked up. The door of the Hotel had opened, and there was a woman standing right beside him – a very large, very fat woman, who seemed to him – shrunk as he was down on the ground, curled up, reduced to an insect's proportions or those of a crawling beetle – to be a giantess, a giantess who had managed to encircle herself in a towelling-fabric bathrobe, pink and frayed. She looked at him in surprise. He mumbled a few words of apology, tried to get back up, smoothed out his raincoat, his trousers, wiped away his tears and rubbed his nose with the back of one hand, sniffed, and then, at last, instinctively striking a pose that resembled someone standing to attention, he introduced himself.

"I am the Investigator."

"So?" the Giantess asked without giving him a chance to continue. Her ample body gave off a slight smell of perspiration, as well as a tepid warmth, the warmth of a bed from which his racket had called her away. Between the badly closed sides of her robe he could see the lighter fabric of a nightdress patterned with faded daisies and daffodils. Her features were chewed up with sleep and she had hurriedly tied up her thick light-red hair by sticking a large pin through it.

"Might you have a room, please?" the Investigator managed to ask. He no longer dared to think that he might be within reach of the end of his grotesque ordeal.

"A room!" the Giantess exclaimed, opening her eyes wide, as though he had put into words a proposal that was preposterous, uncalled-for, obscene even. Once again the Investigator felt his legs threaten to give way beneath him. She looked outraged.

"Yes, a room . . ." he said again, and it was almost an entreaty.

"Do you know what time it is?"

He shrugged pathetically.

"I know," he muttered, without the slightest idea, without the courage to look at his watch, without even the strength to apologise or to embark on an explanation, which, in any case, would hardly have been convincing, and which might have made him seem yet more suspect.

The Giantess thought for a few seconds, grumbling to herself.

"Follow me!" she said at last.

# 6

SHE MADE HIM FILL OUT AN INCALCULABLE NUMBER OF INFORMATION forms, which she then immediately tried to enter into the hard disc of an old computer, but she seemed not to be too comfortable using it, typing with two fingers, frequently hitting the wrong key, even accidentally shutting down the programme five times before she was able to record the data.

Each time she had to start again from the beginning.

Then she handed him the Hotel's regulations – a laminated double page covered with fingerprints, which in places made it opaque and indecipherable – insisting that he read it carefully, out loud, to her, which he did without flinching, trying to be pleasant.

Then she made sure to check that he had retained it all properly and taken in everything that he had read, by asking him a few questions: "Are you allowed to smoke in the rooms?" "From what time to what time is breakfast served – and where?" "May the residents entertain people from outside in their rooms?" "What are you strictly forbidden from disposing of in the toilets?", etc.

As he gave an incorrect answer to her fourteenth question – "Are you allowed to iron personal belongings in your room without notifying the Management in advance?", the Giantess invited him to reread the regulations (which comprised thirty-seven paragraphs) in their entirety. He had to do it, being too afraid that he would be escorted to the door and end up spending the rest of the night out on the street. But finally, since he did nonetheless manage to prevail in this test, the Giantess allowed him to choose one of the keys from the board, after having asked him for some identification and his credit card, which – before he had the chance to protest – she locked in a little safe positioned beneath the board of keys, a procedure that was the subject of paragraph 18, sub-section C of the regulations which, in the event of a guest arriving during the night, gave the Management of Hotel Hope the right to retain his or her documentation and method of payment until the following morning as a precautionary measure.

"Be quick about it. I'm in no mood to hang around for very long. It's 3.16 in the morning, I don't get much of a night, and I'm in a hurry to get back to bed!"

He decided on 14. The Giantess unhooked the key and without a word began to climb the stairs. The Investigator followed her.

He almost stumbled and fell on the first step, as it was of an uncommon height that went against the unconscious memory of his stride. The next, meanwhile, was very low, too low, which also confused him and likewise all but brought him to his knees. So from then on he paid very particular attention, in spite of his tiredness, to each of the steps on the staircase, telling himself that, in any case, there couldn't be as many as fifty of them, since, having chosen room 14, it wouldn't take him long to reach the first floor.

He managed well and congratulated himself on this, as no two steps resembled one another. A staircase like that had to be the product of an unbalanced mind. The problem was also that the Giantess and the Investigator had long passed the first floor, and the two of them did not stop going up, up, up. The Investigator followed the Giantess with some difficulty, gritting his teeth, hauling his suitcase as best he could, taking in each of the floors, step after step, exhausted. The Hotel was beginning to resemble an infinite tower, corkscrewing in on itself, which seemed to be trying to pierce the sky, like a drill whose raison d'être is to make holes in a piece of wood.

Then, brutally, a thought came to him – bright, evident, incontrovertible: he was dead. He had died without realising it. This observation struck him as quite obvious: what other explanation could there be for all this? Maybe it had happened a few hours earlier, when he'd got off the train? Maybe he'd accidentally walked across one of the tracks? Maybe a train had hit him, crushed him, reduced him to nothing? Maybe all that had happened even earlier, while he was coming out of the Head of Department's office, armed with his mission brief: a devastating attack, a cardiac arrest, an irreversible stroke, just after he'd greeted the Accountant who was waiting for her cup of coffee by the automatic dispenser, readjusting her hair and her make-up? Or at home, perhaps? In the morning, getting up, even before he'd stopped his alarm clock vibrating, the hand fixed at 6.15 a.m., an instantaneous death, without any suffering. A long slide. And then nothing else. Or rather – yes – something, this nightmare, which had to be a kind of stress test, an initiation test, a better kind of purgatory: somewhere someone was watching him, he was more and more sure of it. Someone was studying him. Someone was going to decide on his fate.

"Here it is," the Giantess said. "Here's your key." She held the object out to him (it felt very heavy), rearranged the two sides of her bathrobe, brushed her right hand across her forehead, which was flecked with fine drops of sweat, then immediately went back down without even wishing him a goodnight, taking away with her her scent of animal and sleep. The Investigator put the key into the lock, turned it, expecting it not to work.

That was not what happened. He went quickly into the room, put down his suitcase, did not even look for the light switch, groped his way over, ended up touching some piece of furniture that was bed-shaped, collapsed onto it fully clothed and fell asleep, after first spending long minutes breathing like a drowning man saved from the waters by clumsy, fat, red hands.

# 7

A SHIP'S SIREN TORE HIM OUT OF HIS SLUMBER – A HUGE SOUND, which screamed for three or four seconds, stopped, then resumed. He sat up in his bed, felt in vain for a light switch, banged his forehead against an object that was stuck to the wall, which fell noisily. The siren stopped abruptly and then he heard a voice, a voice that was at once close and far away:

"Hello! Hello . . . ? Hello, can you hear me . . . ? Hello?"

Feeling his way, he grabbed the receiver that was hanging at the end of its cable.

"Yes, I can hear you."

"Hello! Can you hear me?" the anxious voice went on.

"I can hear you perfectly. Who are you?" repeated the Investigator, a little more loudly.

"HELLO!!" yelled the voice. "HELLO!!!!"

"Go ahead – I can hear you! I can hear you just fine!"

"Damn it all, is there or isn't there anyone there? I beg you, answer me! Answer me! I'm locked in! I've been locked in!!! I can't get out of this room!" the voice was coming across as more and more desperate.

"I'm here! I'm here," the Investigator said. "I can hear you perfectly well!"

There was another yell at the other end of the line, a crackling and then nothing, save a sharp and intermittent dial tone.

Running his two hands along the wall above the bed, the Investigator finally managed to locate the light switch. The ceiling lamp went on after faltering a few times: it was a circular neon tube, which spread a green light over the room. This was considerably vaster than the Investigator had imagined. The bed on which he was stretched out was lost in a room spanning at least ten metres by seven. For a moment he lay there stunned. With the exception of the bed, the only furniture consisted of a very small cupboard nestled in a corner, and a chair that had been positioned in the middle of the room beneath the ceiling lamp. Nothing else. No bedside table. No desk. The old parquet floor was covered here and there by oriental rugs that had lost all their colour and their patterns. On the back wall, a photographic portrait depicted an old man with a moustache. The Investigator felt he'd seen that face before, but couldn't have sworn as much. It wasn't much like the décor and comfort of a luxury hotel!

The Investigator looked at his watch: 6.47 a.m. The mistake with the telephone had done some good after all. Without it, God only knew what time he would have woken up! But who could he have been, that madman who'd called him?

He got up. He had only slept a few hours. His head hurt, his nose was swollen, hot, sore, running incessantly. He shivered. He noticed that he was still in his raincoat, which had dried a little but which for the most part was completely creased, in his crumpled suit that gave off a strange smell of forest mushrooms, in his shirt that no longer resembled anything and his tie that had wrapped itself three times round his neck. His shoes – which he had also kept on – were still soaked.

He undressed quickly, put his clothes down on the bed, along with his vest and his boxers, then headed towards a door he presumed to be that for the bathroom. The proportions of it staggered him: it was a narrow cupboard. Just as the bedroom was uselessly large, so the bathroom was small, narrow and low-ceilinged, and, what was more, of only questionable hygiene. Hairs in the sink bore witness to a former presence that no-one had bothered to erase. He went in, bending slightly, and couldn't close the door behind him for fear that he would never get it open again. With immense effort, he managed to get himself – standing sideways-on – into what passed for a shower cubicle, and, slipping his hand behind him, but unable to turn around, opened the tap: a burst of icy water gushed out at the level of his shoulder-blades. He couldn't help crying out. He tried blindly to operate the mixer tap, but this time he was sprayed with boiling water. He managed to turn the tap that released the hot water back in the other direction. The Investigator gave up. He forced himself to stand under this torture for nearly thirty seconds, then switched off the tap and twisted himself out of the cubicle.

Thanks to a minute hand towel he dried himself off, and then, looking at himself in a narrow mirror positioned above a sink of

35

similar scale, which returned a deformed, monstrous reflection of himself, he noticed that when he had knocked into the base of the telephone receiver, he had cut his forehead three centimetres across. He had bled badly. He cleaned off the blood. He was left with a deep, open wound, an unsightly gash. You might have thought he had been in a fight and had taken a nasty hit or that someone had tried to knock him out.

With some difficulty he slid out of the bathroom, took his razor out of the suitcase, came back into the narrow little room, got down on all fours to plug the cable into the electric socket that was located, almost diabolically, behind the column that supported the sink, practically at ground level, then he pressed the button on the razor.

Nothing.

He checked that the cable was correctly plugged into the device, tried again.

Nothing.

He looked around the room for another electric socket, eventually found one, half-hidden by the little cupboard, pushed this piece of furniture aside, liberated the socket as well as piles of dust, a few cigarette butts, three used paper handkerchiefs, an old orthodontic brace, pushed the shaver's plug in the socket, switched on the motor: still nothing. His razor refused to work. The Investigator remembered how the previous evening, during his long ramblings, his suitcase had opened and spilled out on the pavement. The razor must have hit the ground, either that or some water had got into the motor. He put it down on the radiator that was beneath the window. This was running at half-strength: it was barely warm.

Of his five spare shirts he took the one that was the least damp, pulled on the other pair of trousers. He had, unfortunately, only one jacket. With the palm of his hand he tried to smooth it out, but the result was far from convincing. Putting on his soggy shoes turned out to be an extremely disagreeable experience, even with socks that were clean and more or less dry. He did up his tie, which insisted on sticking outwards, then with his right hand smoothed down the three locks of hair he still had on top of his head. He was ready to go down for his breakfast.

But first he wanted to get a bit of air into his room, to dispel the thick smell of damp and rain-soaked leather that had invaded it. He drew back the curtains, opened the window – not without difficulty – succeeded in pulling across the rusty metal strip that held the shutters closed from inside and then with the palms of his hands pushed the two flaps at once: they only moved one ludicrous centimetre. The Investigator applied some more pressure, but with the same result. It was incomprehensible. It felt as though the shutters were bumping against something harder than them. He moved closer, looked between their slats, and saw that there were thick breeze blocks, carefully positioned and mortared, preventing them from opening.

He had to accept this unbelievable fact: the window had been bricked up.

# 8

AS HE WALKED DOWN THE STAIRCASE, AFTER HAVING LOOKED FOR a lift that did not exist, the Investigator wondered what it was, this hotel that he had landed in. A hotel which took itself for such a luxury establishment, whose prices were obscenely high and which, in reality, possessed all the distinction of a filthy, condemned old shack.

Seventy-three. That was the number of steps he had walked down. Six floors already, and he still hadn't reached the reception. He clung to this rigorous counting in order to stop himself from thinking of anything. The Hotel was completely silent. The staircase was only lit here and there by a weak bulb that dangled on the wall, making the walk down a precarious experience.

Finally the Investigator reached the ground floor. He had counted nine flights. He had slept in room 14, which was on the ninth floor. The owner was not too bothered about logic. But after all, the Investigator said to himself, was this world he lived in logical? Was logic any more than a purely mathematical notion, a kind of hypothetical premise never yet authenticated by any proof?

There was no-one behind the desk, but there was a ray of light filtering through from below the door that the Giantess had indicated as being the breakfast room. He walked towards it, took the handle, turned it – producing an unpleasant creaking, like a human groan – and pushed the door.

He stopped dead on the threshold.

It was a hall, so large it was almost impossible to see where it ended, but what astonished him the most was that it was absolutely packed. At all the countless tables, he could not see a single free place. Hundreds of people were having their breakfast, and they had all frozen still and interrupted their conversations when he came in. Hundreds of eyes were staring at him. He felt his face turn crimson. He was getting ready to formulate some apology, a few words, perhaps a good morning, but he did not get the chance. After the few seconds' complete silence that accompanied his entrance, the room was once again filled with noise, in fact a thousand noises, a real din of words, of jaws chewing, throats swallowing liquids and bread rolls, the clink of cups, glasses, saucers, the clatter of chairs. He was still lost in his state of surprise when a waiter in a white jacket and black trousers appeared at his side.

"You're in 14?"

"Yes . . ." the Investigator stammered.

"Follow me."

The Waiter had him cross almost half the hall, taking him on a winding path that allowed the Investigator to notice that all the women and men seated at the tables were speaking a foreign language, something Slavonic, unless it was of Scandinavian or Middle Eastern origin.

"Please—" the Waiter said, gesturing towards a free place at a table for four, where the three other places were occupied by low-browed men, with dark skin, their hair thick and black, and who were bent over their cups, drinking and eating greedily.

The Investigator sat down. The Waiter stood ready to take his order.

"A tea, toast and an orange juice, please."

"Tea, yes. Toast and orange juice, no."

"Why not? For the price I'm paying here! Aren't we supposed to be in a four-star hotel?"

"You haven't paid anything yet," the Waiter commented drily, "and the fact that this hotel is four-star doesn't get you absolutely everything, and especially doesn't allow you to behave like someone with such a sense of entitlement."

The Investigator was flabbergasted. He couldn't think of anything to reply. The Waiter got ready to leave but the Investigator held him back.

"I'm sorry, I'd like to ask you a question."

The Waiter said nothing, but nonetheless didn't leave. The Investigator thought there might be some encouragement in this.

"I've only been here since last night, and I thought, well, your colleague, a woman, a large woman, in a robe, she led me to understand that the Hotel was empty, but this morning I see that . . ."

"Tourists. A sudden, massive influx of Tourists."

"Tourists?" asked the Investigator, who was recalling the depressing, charmless streets through which he had walked for hours in the rain and the snow, the endless wall, the grey edifices, the monstrous mass of countless buildings that made up The Firm, the absence of any kind of appeal or any kind of beauty.

"This town attracts a large number of Tourists," the Waiter retorted, and took advantage of this devastating riposte to hurry off.

The Investigator unfolded his napkin and looked at his neighbours, who were still eating and drinking.

"Morning!" the Investigator called out to them.

None of them replied, nor even looked at him. The Waiter returned. He put two breakfast rusks and a cup of black coffee down in front of him, then left, before the Investigator had the time to point out that this was not what he had ordered at all.

# 9

THE RUSKS TASTED OF SOIL. AS FOR THE BLACK COFFEE, IT WAS
without a doubt the bitterest that the Investigator had ever drunk
in his life, and even the sugar he added in copious quantities wasn't
able to sweeten it. His three neighbours were devouring cheese
omelettes, cold meats, smoked fish, large gherkins in vinegar, apple
and cinnamon pastries, soft bread rolls packed with raisins and
almonds, fresh fruit. They were drinking grapefruit juice and
pineapple juice as well as black tea whose delicious scent – full-
flavoured and smoky – reached the Investigator's nostrils.

Their conversation was rattling along, but the Investigator could
not understand a word of it. None of them paid him any attention.

He forced himself to drink his coffee, thinking that the hot
liquid would do him good. He had not stopped blowing his
nose and he felt feverish. From time to time he would look up at
the hall, trying to spot the Giantess, but she never appeared. Only
Waiters, four or five of them, who might have been taken for
brothers they so resembled one another, small, slightly round, their
bald skulls, serving the tables. The Tourists – he had resolved to
call them that – were making an unbelievable din. They were

women and men of about forty, modestly dressed, who threw themselves on the abundant food that had been placed in front of them, eating messily. He noticed that he was the only person to have been offered the rudimentary breakfast he was being forced to swallow, and when a Waiter went past him he asked whether he too might have an omelette and a fruit juice.

"Are you part of the group?"

"No, I'm . . ."

"You're in 14?"

"Yes."

"I'm sorry, it's quite impossible."

"But that's ridiculous! Couldn't you at least give me a little jam, or even just some butter – if it's a question of money I'll pay extra . . . ?!"

"Don't keep insisting. Here money isn't the answer to every problem."

The Waiter was already some distance away now and the Investigator – outraged – still hadn't got over his surprise. In his head he ran through all the articles of the internal regulations that he'd read over twice on his arrival, and couldn't remember anything in it relating to some kind of discrimination regarding breakfast. He promised himself that he'd say something about it to one of the Management staff as soon as he could.

Time was passing: attached to a wall, a huge clock, which made the noise of a hammer striking an anvil, punctuating each advance of its hand over the second notches with a resounding "clack!", reminded him of it. He shouldn't dawdle. They had to be waiting for him and getting impatient. He grabbed the cup to finish his coffee, but just as he was bringing it to his lips his neighbour knocked him with his elbow. The coffee tipped over his jacket and his trousers. The Investigator swore: two dark brown stains spread across the light fabric. The man who had caused this disaster did not apologise. He continued eating and talking to the other two, who were also behaving as though he did not exist.

The Investigator got up and headed quickly towards a door above which there was a sign marking the toilets. He was quite beside himself. He was beginning to have more than enough of this, and wondered whether he ought not just return on the earliest train. But what could he have said to the Head of Department to explain his premature return, before the Investigation had even taken place, before it had even begun? That he'd wandered through the town for hours in utterly foul weather? That the Hotel seemed odd? That the breakfast they'd served him hadn't been suitable? That the coffee was appalling? That the staff behaved inexcusably? That his table companions didn't say a word to him?

No, better to be patient.

The corridor in which he found himself once he had left the room came to a dead end a dozen or so metres further on. He saw two doors in the left-hand wall. On the first, a pictogram showed a female silhouette; he went on to the second, but the picture on this one was just the same. He retreated, thinking he must have made some mistake. No. He had seen it right. Both doors were marked as ladies' toilets. He felt his heart begin to run away with itself. He was still being mocked.

He glanced right and then left, and even upwards, too. No-one. He did not hesitate a second and went straight in. The washroom was deserted. He went over to a basin, got some hot water flowing, rummaged in his pocket to take out a handkerchief that wasn't there. Nor in his other pocket.

There was a fabric towel attached to a roller. He tried delicately to unhook it. Without any success. He pulled on the fabric, pulled some more, pulled harder. The towel tore and the wall screws for the roller came loose from the plaster, which crazed over with cracks all across it. He moistened the towel, and rubbed energetically at the two coffee stains. After a few minutes, he thought they might have blurred a little: they had lost their dark colour. While lighter, they were in compensation now more spread out. The Investigator threw the torn towel into a rubbish bin, pushed it right down, covering it over with paper, and left the washroom.

When he pushed open the door to the breakfast room the noise had completely stopped: the Tourists had vanished. Not a single one was left. The tables were cleared and clean. There was no leftover mess at all! How was this possible, given that he'd been out of the room for no more than four minutes?

The chairs had been tidied away neatly. He looked at the place where he had been: the coffee cup was still there, as well as the second rusk, which he hadn't completely finished, and on the chair, just slightly askew, out of line with the table, his raincoat.

It was the only place where anything had been left.

The Waiters themselves had become invisible.

The Investigator ran to his place. He wanted to get out as quickly as possible, out of this hall, out of this Hotel, to get outside and take deep breaths of fresh air, to feel that freshness on his brow, on the back of his neck, in his lungs, in his brain so to speak, his brain which had had such a strain put on it, so much so that the Investigator wondered whether it might not suddenly burst. But while he was putting on his raincoat, and returning to that unpleasant feeling of dampness, he heard a loud voice from behind him, calling out from some distance away:

"You aren't finishing your breakfast?"

## 10

HE FROZE AND, VERY SLOWLY, FEAR IN HIS BELLY, HE TURNED. There was a man walking towards him. A man he had never seen before, who was neither a Waiter nor a Tourist. As the man approached, his silhouette became clearer, as did his face. He might have been the same age as the Investigator, and the same build. He was smiling.

"You aren't finishing your breakfast?" the man said again, in a pleasant voice, gesturing towards the cup and the rusk.

"I'm not very hungry anymore," the Investigator mumbled, "and I'm already late."

"Late . . . ? If you say so! Personally, I find that in life one is often early, and that death comes all too quickly. Come on, sit down, finish your breakfast in peace, don't worry about me."

The Investigator hadn't the strength to protest. Beneath his affability the man was giving off something commanding. He sat down without removing his raincoat, of which he had only put on a single sleeve. The man took the chair opposite him, looked at him attentively.

"Did you sleep well?"

"I arrived very late, and—"

"I know," the man interrupted him. "You had a short night. But please, eat, just pretend I'm not here."

The man gestured towards the rusk. The Investigator took hold of it reluctantly and began to nibble on it.

"Let me introduce myself," said the man. "I am the Policeman."

"The Policeman . . ." the Investigator repeated fearfully, and having put down his rusk shook the hand the man held out to him.

"Precisely. And as for you, you are . . ."

"Well, that is," the Investigator began to reply, his voice choking a little, and sweating copiously, "I'm . . . I'm . . ."

"You're?"

"I've come to carry out an Investigation at The Firm."

"An Investigation? Well, fancy that! An Investigation! And I didn't even know about it?"

The Policeman was still wearing his good-natured smile, but his eyes didn't leave the Investigator's.

"It's not a police enquiry, nothing like that," stammered the Investigator. "Don't misunderstand me! It's only a simple administrative procedure. The Firm experienced a significant – and to speak frankly, unusual – rate of suicides this past year and they've asked me to—"

"Suicides?" the man interrupted him.

"Yes. Suicides."

"How many?"

"About twenty."

"Twenty!? And nobody notified me? But this is unbelievable! I am the Policeman, there are serial suicides a few steps from my office and I don't know anything about it! When you say about twenty, how many do you mean exactly?"

More and more uneasy, the Investigator was still gripping hold of his rusk. He was sure he had a fever now. His head hurt. His eyes stung. The back of his neck had tensed up. His nose was burning and painful, like the scar on his forehead. His whole body was making him suffer. The Policeman rummaged in the right-hand pocket of his jacket, then in the left, and took from it a yellow and blue tube, which he held out to the Investigator.

"Take two of these."

"What are they?"

"You have a headache, don't you?"

"How did you know?"

"I know everything, that's my job. Your arrival yesterday, your wait at a bar, the argument about the grog, your insistence at the Guardhouse, your dazed wandering, your knocking at the Hotel door, followed by your inability to reply to the simplest questions regarding the internal regulations, and this morning your rude comments about breakfast. There's nothing I don't know. I've been given very thorough briefing notes. I am the Policeman. I know. You, who are the Investigator, you don't know, you seek. I'm a long way ahead of you. Two, I said."

"Excuse me?"

"Two tablets. Go on, you've still got a drop of coffee left."

The Investigator held the tube of medicine nestled in the palm of his hand. He hesitated to open it. The Policeman gave a great laugh.

"Oh, but you really needn't be afraid! I'm the Policeman, not the Murderer! Each to his role! And yours, yours is to be the Investigator, right? And if you follow the prescribed dosage, there's no risk at all."

The Investigator nodded slowly.

"There now. All clear! Just pretend I'm not here." With these words the Policeman looked down, inspecting his hands ostentatiously, as though to prove that he was not watching the Investigator's movements. The latter, completely thrown by the sudden arrival of this character, didn't know how to react to him. He ended up opening the tube, taking out two tablets, which were also, like the tube, yellow and blue, looking at them carefully, trying to breathe but his nose was so blocked that he could no longer smell a thing. He hesitated a little longer, then placed them on his tongue, closed his eyes and swallowed them down, drinking what was left of the foul black coffee.

The Policeman had looked up again and gone back to watching him. He was still smiling.

"Well then, these suicides. How many exactly?"

"Twenty-three. But there is some doubt about one of those. It isn't known whether this person ended his own life or whether it was an accident. Gas."

"Wow, that's wild – gas! You die and sometimes you take other people along with you. Is that what happened?"

"No. He lived alone in a bungalow."

"Shame . . ."

"Excuse me?"

"Nothing. Forget it."

There was a silence. The Policeman seemed to be weighing up what the Investigator had just told him about the suicides. He had not lost his smile. He gave a slight gesture with his hand, as if to sweep that all aside and move on to another matter.

"You must think you've landed in a pretty unique place, right?"

"Well, that is, I must confess—"

"Tsk, tsk . . ." interrupted the Policeman, who gave a great laugh, "you have nothing whatsoever to confess. Our conversation isn't a cross-examination – relax!"

The Investigator wasn't sure exactly why, but as a man who had absolutely nothing to blame himself for, he suddenly felt a great weight lifted off him. He began to laugh with the Policeman. It did him good. Ah yes, how that laughter did him good, with this thoroughly benign man who was also surprised at the way things had turned out.

"To tell you the truth," the Investigator went on, "would you believe I don't understand any of it? I feel I've been living in a kind of nightmare since I set foot in this town, or, rather, that I'm the victim of some gigantic hoax. Everything seems to have been set up in order to prevent me from doing what I have to do . . ."

"The Investigation of the suicides?"

"Exactly! It's as if – and what I'm about to tell you will sound ridiculous – it's as if everything here in this town, even the layout of the streets, the lack of signposts, the climate, everything was conspiring to stop me carrying out my Investigation, or at least to delay it as much as possible. I've never seen the like. And this hotel! Has there ever been a hotel like it?"

The Policeman thought about this carefully. His round face still wore its smile, but his eyes seemed to narrow as if with an intense effort of concentration.

"I felt the same as you when I first arrived. I haven't been here long. We're constantly shunted about from post to post, and naturally we can't complain, we haven't the right. I wondered what I was doing here, who could possibly have made the preposterous decision to get me sent to this place, and what for. I did indeed know that I was the Policeman, but no-one had given me any further specifications about what it was I had to do, what role they wanted me to play. Very odd. Very, very odd. And then, well, I don't really know how to put this, but I could sense a very clear . . . presence."

"As if there was someone watching you?"

"Precisely. Exactly so! But I was never able to catch anyone."

"It's like that for me, I've had that feeling since yesterday evening."

"But, well . . . you end up getting used to it! That's what a man does, he adapts, right? And nowadays aren't we constantly being watched, wherever we are, whatever we're doing?"

The two men drifted into a reverie, but the sound of a telephone rang out. Both of them at once began to rummage hurriedly through their pockets, which made them laugh, but the Investigator remembered that his was completely out of battery. The Policeman removed his phone from his jacket, a model the Investigator had never seen before, oblong, with only a single button, which he pressed, gesturing to excuse himself.

"Yes?"

The Investigator felt relieved. This man sitting in front of him, who in some respects resembled him greatly, gave him some comfort.

"Hang on . . . hang on . . ." the Policeman said, drawing a notebook and a pen from his pocket. His face had just lost its smile.

"At what time, you say?"

He jotted down a few notes.

"You're sure?"

The Investigator looked away so as not to make him uncomfortable.

"Very well. Thank you for letting me know."

The Policeman pressed the only button on the telephone and slipped it gently into one of his pockets. He read over the meticulous notes he had just taken, all the while scratching the back of his neck. Then he shut his notebook sharply. His eyes were now like those of a fox, very small, ochre-coloured and shining.

"Nothing serious, I hope?" asked the Investigator breezily.

"That depends for whom," replied the Policeman coolly. He went on, in a dry, metallic voice, weighing up each of his words:

"Can you explain to me why, at 7.21 this morning, you entered the ladies' toilet, and for what reason while there you deliberately destroyed a towel, along with its holder – made of wood and metal – and all with unjustifiable savagery?"

The rusk that the Investigator was still holding between his fingers exploded into a thousand pieces, and at the same time he seemed to feel two hands yanking him down into a bottomless abyss.

## 11

IT WAS ALREADY SOME WAY INTO THE MORNING WHEN HE WAS finally able to leave Hotel Hope.

The Policeman had detained him for nearly two hours, and during these two hours he had had to reply to a flood of brusquely asked questions, some of them repeated several times at a few minutes' interval in order to be sure that his answers remained constant. Three times he had had to explain his tiniest acts and movements since he had got up, the phone call that had woken him, and the bricked-up window – "I shall check that!" the Policeman had said then, almost threateningly – down to his counting of the stairs, the huge presence of Tourists in the breakfast room – "Tourists? Really . . . ? First I've heard about it!" chuckled the Policeman – and finally the incident in the toilets.

The Policeman also – with the greatest attention – insisted on examining the scar on the Investigator's forehead. In order to do so, he extracted a pair of surgical gloves. Then he stood up and ordered the Investigator to accompany him to the toilets in order to carry out a reconstruction.

"A what?!"

"You understood me perfectly."

"But you must be mad! A reconstruction for a torn towel? What is this world we're in? I don't have time to waste on your childishness. I've got a job waiting for me. I have an Investigation to carry out. People are dead. Men and women have committed suicide, I don't believe you grasp what it means, this business of committing suicide, and I've got to work out why. I have to discover why in such a short space of time, within the same firm, within The Firm, people were so desperate that they preferred to end it all rather than resort to a Psychologist, rather than opening up to the Occupational Health Doctor, requesting a meeting with the Director of Human Resources, confiding in their colleagues or a member of their family, or even calling the number for one of the many organisations that help people in distress! And you put these spokes in my wheels, detaining me because of trifles, you question me for more than an hour about a damaged towel, about damage which would never have happened if this hotel had provided the most basic services that a customer is entitled to demand, you make me waste my time, and—"

"Who am I?" the Policeman interrupted him.

"I beg your pardon?"

"Who am I?"

"You're . . . You told me you were the Policeman."

"Precisely. And?"

"And what?"

"And what?! Are the orders of the Policeman to be questioned?"

The Investigator opened his mouth, felt his throat dry up and the words die in it. His shoulders sank.

"Let's get it over with as quickly as possible," he sighed.

The Policeman asked him to follow him to the toilets. The reconstruction was ready to take place. It would take twenty-seven minutes. The Investigator would have to carry out the same movements and make the same gestures as before. The Policeman watched him from different angles, jotted down notes, drew an extremely precise diagram, walked in long strides to measure out the space, the distances, used his mobile phone to take a few photographs of the broken towel-holder, and of the torn towel, which he had extracted from the rubbish bin only after having put on a new pair of surgical gloves, and of the Investigator, in close-up, face-on and in profile. He asked a number of questions, checked that the stains on the Investigator's trousers and jacket had not disappeared, and when at last he seemed convinced that the Investigator was not hiding anything from him and that what he had told him had been the exact truth, he asked him to follow him to his premises.

"Your premises? What premises?"

"My office, if you prefer. Did you think I was going to let you leave without taking a statement?"

"A state—"

The Policeman was already off. The Investigator had no choice but to follow at his heels. The two of them left the toilets. The Policeman closed the door behind them, and to the Investigator's absolute astonishment sealed it shut. Then they crossed the vast breakfast hall, passed the reception – still deserted – and stopped

57

outside a door to its right, on which a sign read, "No entry except to staff". The Policeman took a key from his pocket, turned it in the lock, opened the door and asked the Investigator to step inside.

It was a broom cupboard – inside there were a large number of buckets, floor cloths, sponges, dustpans, cleaning products as well as a very big vacuum-cleaner. In one corner, on two trestles, two planks of wood laid side by side held a mechanical type-writer.

"I can't stand computers," exclaimed the Policeman, who had noticed the Investigator looking sceptically at it. "Computers de-humanise relationships."

The Policeman held out a pink plastic bucket to the Investigator, who took it without understanding. The Policeman himself took another, which was blue, turned it over and sat on it.

"Go on, don't be afraid, they're quite solid and actually very comfortable. I haven't had my chairs delivered yet."

The Policeman inserted a sheet of paper into the typewriter's roller. He performed this movement with the greatest meticulous-ness. What was more, he repeated the exercise three times because the sheet seemed to him to have gone in just slightly askew.

"And what if I've been dealing with a madman?" the Investigator asked himself, suddenly. "Maybe he's no more a policeman than I am God Almighty? He never showed me his card. His office is in a hotel, and what office is that? A common storeroom! Yes, he's a madman! Why didn't it occur to me sooner?"

This thought gave him back his confidence. He almost burst out laughing, but he restrained himself. Better not to give anything away, to continue in the madman's game a few moments longer, and then clear off as fast as he could. He would have plenty of free time this evening to complain to the Hotel Management about the time this sick man – who was surely just a common cleaning operative suffering from depression – had made him waste.

"We're all set!" exclaimed the Policeman, who had resumed his broad smile on seeing the white sheet of paper, perfectly horizontal, precisely parallel to the upper edge of the typewriter's roller.

"I'm all yours," the Investigator replied.

## 12

A LARGE SUN WAS WHITENING THE ALREADY PALE SKY. IT WAS MILD, almost hot, quite unlike the temperature of the previous night. The Investigator blinked and stopped still for a moment on the Hotel steps, incredulous, glad and relieved to be out at last, even though he was terribly late. He felt a little better. Was that the effect of the medication the Policeman had given him?

Having been so badly pushed about and knocked off-balance for these past few hours, he was once again ready to go back to being the Investigator: scrupulous, professional, alert, rigorous and methodical, a man who didn't allow himself to be surprised or bothered by circumstances or the individuals he came across in the course of his investigations.

A human wave walked along the pavement past him in perfect silence: a quick, thick crowd who filed by at full speed, as though carried on a great in-draught of air. It was made up of women and men of all ages, but who all walked at the same speed, not speaking to one another, their eyes on the ground or straight ahead of them. What was particularly unusual was that on the pavement closest to him the Crowd moved towards the right, while on the other pavement, the one on the far side of the road, the opposite was happening, as though someone somewhere had established a direction of movement that nobody dared to infringe.

The only thing to be heard was the very quiet sound of the vehicles. They circulated at walking speed, all in the same direction, left to right. It was a magnificent traffic jam! The cars proceeded extremely slowly, but in absolutely perfect order, and the Investigator could not make out any trace of annoyance on the faces of the drivers, who looked straight ahead and seemed to be bearing their troubles patiently. No horns either, no insults, just the rumbling of the engines, elegant, almost subdued, and volatile.

The rhythm of the Town had decidedly changed. Deserted at night, during the day it showed itself to have a liveliness that was industrious and focused, regular, fluid, which whipped the Investigator up and provided him with a sudden burst of energy. It is true, the density of the Crowd, and of the traffic, was somewhat surprising given the desolation and emptiness of the night, but after the disconcerting events he had just been through and the peculiar characters he had been dealing with, he did feel all the same as though he were falling back into a kind of normality that he was glad to accept, while ignoring any awkward questions.

He still needed to find his way. He had not wanted to ask the Policeman for directions, sure that he – Policeman or not – would have taken advantage of this to ask him an infinite number of questions and perhaps even to place him under custody in his tiny room.

The Investigator examined the buildings he could see: huge warehouses, a series of metal or stone hangars, all of them occupied by offices, administrative premises, immense covered car parks, storage workshops, laboratories, metal chimneys from which an almost transparent smoke was escaping. The heterogeneity of these constructions was really only noticeable because they all belonged to the operations of The Firm, as demonstrated by the outer wall that encircled them, marking out a boundary, but also creating links, connections, bridges, bonds between them, assimilating them into the cells or the limbs of a single vast body.

The whole Town seemed to be encompassed in The Firm, as though it were in a gradual process of expansion that nothing could stop and had stretched out beyond its original limits, swallowing up its boundaries, digesting them, assimilating them as it instilled its own identity into them. All this gave off a mysterious power that made the Investigator momentarily dizzy. As someone who had long been aware that his position in the world and in society was a matter of the very tiniest significance, he was discovering – faced with this landscape of The Firm's immoderate size – a new kind of unease, that of his anonymity. Besides knowing that he was nothing, he suddenly discovered that he was nobody. This thought, while it didn't worry him, did nonetheless enter him like an odd little worm penetrating an already fragile fruit.

But his reverie was brought abruptly to an end when he noticed, about two hundred metres away to his left, on the other side of the road, a recess in the outer wall that gave him a sort of dizzy turn.

Yes, that very wide-open angle, that break in the wall's continuity, there was no doubt about it: it really was the way in. The way in to The Firm. The way in, where the Guardhouse was. And to think, the Hotel was barely a minute away: it must have taken him hours to get from one to the other, God alone knew by what impossible route. It was enough to make you want to laugh. The Investigator felt practically euphoric.

He went down the four steps to the pavement and looked about him for a pedestrian crossing to be able to get over to the far side. But even trying to examine his surroundings as best he could, crouching down till his face was at ground level in order to try and make out those meaningful white strips between the legs of the passers-by and under the wheels of the cars, going back up the four steps, then raising himself up on his tiptoes in order to try and see as far as he possibly could to find a red light, he found nothing.

The Investigator stopped to think for a few moments, and made a decision: he had wasted enough time already, he said to himself, and decided to breach the tide of cars, which was not going to be difficult at all given their speed.

# 13

THE FIRST PROBLEM, WHICH TO TELL THE TRUTH HE HAD QUITE underestimated, was getting to the edge of the pavement, that is, getting through the compact, moving mass of men and women walking past him, a strip two or three metres wide, but which was dense, mobile, calmly hostile.

At first he made some effort to speak all kinds of words of apology out loud, explaining with discreet gestures that he would like to get by, showing himself as polite as could be, and even so, nobody stopped, nor did anyone move in order that he might be able to slip between the bodies. The women and the men walking past did not look at him. Many of them had their ears covered by helmets or headphones, while others – there were many of these, too – were using a one-button telephone, identical to the Policeman's, on which they were writing messages or receiving calls.

The Investigator said to himself that in such conditions he would have to resign himself to forcing his way through, elbowing his way, without thinking too much about it, even if it meant treading on a few toes or shoving two or three people. In any case he'd had enough of nobody paying him any attention. He took a deep breath and threw himself in.

It was a strange kind of crush, which unfolded in a way that was not at all aggressive, but in a kind of violence that was silent, extreme and disconcerting: a jumble of bodies without any crying out, without any insults, without unnecessary movements, without hatred. The Investigator felt at once as though he were swimming in a torrent of stormy waters and as though he were being pushed around by a bulldozer made of supple, soft shapes. He fought off hands, he clung, scratched, grabbed, pushed people apart, shouted, cried out, exclaimed, groaned, begged, even debased himself. He deployed an energy drawn up from his very depths. At last he reached the far side of the pavement.

The effort had in fact been as intense as the distance travelled had been short. He was breathless, and he realised that in the struggle his raincoat, which had already resembled an old, badly ironed bed sheet, had suffered greatly: his right pocket was torn and the fabric hung down, like a large dog-ear, supple and pathetic. He didn't waste any time on regret, as he still had to cross the tide of vehicles ahead of him.

He raised his hand to the driver of the first vehicle to his left, so that he might understand he intended to cross, but no sooner had he taken two or three steps onto the road, just enough to edge round the front of this first car and begin to slip between the next two, than a thousand horns suddenly rang out in a din that petrified the Investigator.

The noise was so immoderate that he wondered whether it was actually real. He reopened his eyes, which he had closed in a sort of reflex a few seconds earlier: all the cars were quite still. In each of them, the driver, man or woman, was leaning angrily on his or her horn, and above all, above all, each of these drivers, each of the dozens of drivers, hundreds of drivers, was looking at him – him, the Investigator – suddenly motionless between the vehicles.

A cold sweat ran down the back of his neck. Abruptly the sound of the horns stopped. But that same moment thousands of voices, blended, woven-together, united voices rose up from the pavements in an extraordinary hubbub. It was as though an entire stadium had come together to yell in unison. And, here again, all the men and all the women who, just moments earlier, had been walking in order and in silence, at an even, regular pace, occupied with their thoughts, their music, their telephone conversations, without the slightest concern for the world surrounding them, had stopped and all the men and all the women were looking at him and shouting at him, shouting words that were rendered inaudible because they were knocking together, crunching, smashing against one another, all distorted by the ricocheting of their crushed-together syllables. He panicked, faltered, barely caught himself, leaning on the bonnet of a car, and hastily retraced his steps and set foot back on the pavement that he had left less than a minute before.

He was trembling. Now nobody was interested in him any longer. On the road the cars rolled on, at walking pace, their drivers staring straight ahead. On the far side everyone had likewise resumed their walk. Everything was back in order. But what order was it?

Imperceptibly, the Crowd was pulling him along in its movement. He could not resist. His legs, even without his brain having taken a decision, were imitating the rhythm of the other legs that surrounded them. He, too, was walking now, and in the direction dictated by the Group, despite the fact that this was the wrong direction, as it made him head to the right, while the way in to The Firm, the Guardhouse, was over there, a few hundred metres away, to the left.

## 14

THEY WERE STRANGE, THOSE FEW MOMENTS, CERTAINLY THE strangest he had experienced since arriving in the Town, this involuntary drifting. The Investigator surrendered and allowed himself to be carried like a wisp of straw on the great current of a river. For the first time in his existence he gave up thinking of himself as an individual with a will, with choice in his actions, living in a country that guaranteed each of its citizens their fundamental freedoms, so fundamental that most of the time everyone, including the Investigator, enjoyed them without even being fully aware of them. Dissolved in this huge moving mass of mute pedestrians, he slipped by, he stopped thinking, refused to analyse the situation, did not try to fight it. It was rather as though he had partially surrendered his body to enter another body, which was vast and limitless.

How long did it last? Who could say? In any case, not the Investigator, that much was certain. He did not know much of anything anymore. He had almost – as though stunned by a violent psychotropic drug – forgotten his very reason for existing. He continued to be, but only weakly. He was losing his density.

It became chillier again, and then brutally colder. The sky

wrapped itself in a grey veil from which a few flakes soon began to escape. These fleeting, frozen little specks, falling on the Investigator's head, brought him back to his present situation. He shuddered, and then noticed that above the heads of the crowd he could see the sign for the Hotel, his Hotel, the Hotel Hope. Finally he told himself that his senses had been completely routed. Having thought that the Crowd had been carrying him along for hours, he had, in fact, travelled only a short distance.

And yet one detail called out to him. Was this really the same hotel? The same sign? Something was different. The Hotel was indeed in its position on the other side of the road, between two buildings that he was also able to identify categorically. On the other side of the road. On the other si—! But of course! That's what was different! If the Hotel was on the other side, it was because he was no longer on the same pavement, so it was because at some point he had swapped pavements, and was now walking on the side of the road where The Firm was! And what was more, yes, over there, a bit further on, on his left, there it was! He could even make out the Guardhouse.

He'd have to be quick about it, slip all the way to the left of the chain of humans in such a way that in just a few moments he might escape from the stream of the Crowd, leave the mass, go back to being an isolated, single human being. A few steps more, a few metres more, just don't miss the exit, just don't get obstructed at the last moment by some hidden individual coming from behind . . .

Phew! He'd done it.

# 15

BY DAY THE GUARDHOUSE SEEMED MUCH LESS HOSTILE THAN AT night. In fact it was only a simple building, plain, almost ugly, but with nothing at all military about it. He didn't need to ring on the intercom for someone to answer him. He just had to get as close to the window as possible, to where it had two dozen little holes arranged in a circle, and bend down a bit to address a middle-aged man, not much hair, a chubby face, the Guard, dressed in white like a Laboratory Technician or a Chemist, and who was waiting on the other side of the glass with a smile.

"Hello!" said the Investigator, feeling as though he was finally going to speak to someone who would listen.

"Hello," the Guard replied, pleasantly.

"I am the Investigator."

The Guard was still smiling, but the Investigator could tell his expression had changed. The Guard was staring at him. This lasted a few seconds, then he consulted the large register open in front of him. He seemed not to find anything, looked at the previous pages, running from line to line with the help of his index finger. At last he stopped at one of them, tapped three times on it.

"Your arrival was expected yesterday at five p.m."

"Just so," the Investigator replied, "but I was significantly delayed."

"Would you have a piece of identification on you, please?" the Guard asked.

"Of course!"

The Investigator sunk his hand into the inside pocket of his jacket, found nothing there, rummaged in the other pocket, started to pale, patted down his raincoat, then suddenly remembered that he'd given his I.D. papers as well as his credit card to the Giantess, whom he'd watched place them in the Hotel safe. He had completely forgotten to retrieve them in the morning.

"I'm sorry," he said, "I've left everything in my hotel. Hotel Hope, I'm sure you know it, it's a few hundred metres from here. On the other side of the road."

These words had dented the Guard's genial expression. He seemed to be thinking. The Investigator tried to maintain his broadest smile as if to convince him of his honesty.

"Give me a few moments."

The Guard closed the register, cut off the microphone that connected him to the outside, picked up a telephone and dialled a number. He must have got through to his interlocutor quite quickly as the Investigator saw him speaking. The conversation went on for a while. The Guard opened the register again, pointed to the line on which the Investigator's arrival time was written, argued at some length, seemed to reply to countless questions, looked closely at the

Investigator, all the while talking, perhaps describing him, and then, at last, hung up the telephone and reconnected the microphone.

"Someone is coming to fetch you. You can wait behind the security barrier to your right."

The Investigator thanked the Guard and headed for the place that he had indicated to him.

The chevaux-de-frise, the rolls of barbed wire, the portcullises and the chicanes had all been taken away. All that remained was a large automated metal barrier, which barred entry to The Firm. Beside it stood a Sentry dressed in a grey paramilitary uniform, with a cap the same colour, his waist adorned with a broad belt to which several objects were attached: a truncheon, a tear-gas grenade, an electric pistol, a pair of handcuffs, a bunch of keys, a mobile telephone, a flashlight, a knife in its sheath and a walkie-talkie. He was also equipped with an earpiece and a small mic attached to the lapel of his jacket.

When he saw the Investigator approach the barrier, he left his post and took a few slow steps towards him, in order to block his passage, but right away the earpiece and the little mic crackled. The Sentry stopped, froze, listened to what someone was telling him, and simply replied, "Roger!"

He was ignoring the Investigator. He was two heads taller than him and his eyes were lost on the rooftops in the distance. The Investigator was uneasy again: really, to think how he must look! He was unshaven, his forehead was crossed by a sizeable and swollen wound, his nose was raw and dripped non-stop, the torn pocket of his completely crumpled raincoat hung down his side, his still wet shoes resembled little bits of badly tanned animal-hide, and he struggled hard to mask the two large coffee stains on his jacket and trousers with the lapels of his raincoat.

A tramp, that's what I must look like . . . Maybe even a drunk, even though I've never touched a drop of alcohol in my life, he thought. The Sentry's outfit, in contrast, was impeccable: not a crease, not a stain, not a snag. His perfectly waxed shoes scorned all the flakes that fell on them. The man was freshly shaven. Everything about him was clean and new. It was as though he'd just come out of his packaging.

"What weather!" the Investigator said with a little smile, but the Sentry did not reply. He was more sad than hurt. Did he count for so little? Was he so insignificant? The effect of the two tablets he'd swallowed with the awful coffee was beginning to blur. A great weariness ran through his whole body, while each of his bones was becoming a point of pain. His head had positioned itself in a vice, and a fearsome hand was gradually clamping down on his temples. He was hot. He was cold. He shivered, sweated, sneezed, coughed, choked, coughed again.

"Keep your germs to yourself, we really have no need for them right now!"

# 16

COMPLETELY TAKEN UP WITH HIS SNEEZING, HE HAD NOT NOTICED the arrival of the man who had just addressed those words to him so briskly.

"You're the Investigator?"

The Investigator nodded, almost reluctantly, while blowing his nose.

"I am the Guide. I will take you to the Manager. I shan't shake your hand, don't take it the wrong way. Here, this is for you."

The Guide could have been about his age. Not very tall, wearing an elegant grey suit, with a somewhat greasy face, without much hair left on his head. He held out a bag to the Investigator, in which he discovered a number of objects: a large white overall, a safety helmet the same colour, a pen, a key-ring adorned with the photograph of an old man with a moustache – the same man whose framed photograph had been hanging on the wall of the hotel room? – a notebook and a small plastic flag both bearing the logo of The Firm, as well as a badge on which was written, in bold characters: "External Element".

"It's the traditional welcome pack. May I ask you please to put on the overall right away, to clip your badge onto the upper left pocket and put the helmet on your head."

"Of course," the Investigator said, as though all this seemed quite natural to him. The overall was far too big, and the helmet too small. As for the badge, it was just right.

"Would you follow me?"

The Investigator didn't need to be asked twice. The serious business would at last be able to begin. He was glad to be wearing this overall, large though it was, which hid the state of dilapidation of his outfit, and the helmet brought a gentle warmth to his skull, as though a friendly hand were stroking it, and shielding it from the snow which was falling ever more thickly. He was recovering his strength.

"You don't wear them?" the Investigator asked.

"Excuse me?"

"A helmet and overall. You don't wear them?"

"No, they're quite useless, to tell the truth, but absolutely compulsory for External Elements. We never compromise on regulations. Please be careful to keep to the line!"

They followed a red line painted onto the ground. Parallel to this there was also a yellow line, a green line and a blue line. The Investigator took advantage of the moment to seek clarification of The Firm's activities.

"That's an enormous question," the Guide began, "and I'm not the person best placed to answer you. I don't know it all. In fact I don't know all that much. The Firm covers so many activities:

communications, engineering, water treatment, renewable energy, nuclear chemistry, petroleum industries, asset valuation, pharmaceutical research, nanotechnology, gene therapy, food processing, banking, insurance, mine prospecting, concrete, real estate, storage and consolidation of non-conventional data, arms, development aid, micro-credit loans, education and training, textiles, plastics manufacturing, publishing, public buildings and works, heritage conservation, investment and taxation advice, agriculture, logging, mental analysis, entertainment, surgery, assistance for disaster victims, and other things I'm forgetting, of course! You see, I'm not sure there's a single sector of activity developed by mankind that doesn't depend directly or indirectly on The Firm, or on one of its subsidiaries. Hang on, we're here."

The Investigator did not manage to digest the itemised list the Guide had given him. He would never have suspected that The Firm covered all those fields, and he found it hard to imagine how such a thing was possible. For a moment he felt he was going to be left all alone to face this thousand-headed creature and the thought made him panic.

They were approaching a conical glass building, and the Investigator noticed that the yellow, green and blue lines were slanting off towards the right, while the red line led right up to the entrance to this building.

"If you wouldn't mind . . ."

The Guide opened the door for him, and the two of them went in. There was a staircase that climbed up from floor to floor, winding round on itself, a bit like in the Hotel, but this one seemed to be made up entirely of steps that were all the same height. Behind the frosted glass doors, it was possible to make out some motionless silhouettes, people of indeterminate sex, who looked as though they were sitting at their desks, opposite rhomboid shapes that might have been computers. The atmosphere was quite silent, almost meditative.

"I'll ask you to give me just a moment, I'll inform the Manager. If you would care to sit and wait." The Guide pointed towards three seats behind a low table on which a number of brochures were arranged.

"I've had a Colleague prepare a set of documents for you to look at, which will give you an idea of The Firm's social policies, how it operates and the constant concern The Firm shows for the well-being of its employees."

The Investigator thanked him, and the Guide began to climb the stairs. His steps echoed as though on the flagstones of a cathedral, and the outline of his body dwindled, but remained visible thanks to the transparent steps of bluish, azure glass, as he made his way skywards up the great spiral.

The Investigator quickly discovered how uncomfortable the chair he had chosen was. As though the seat were tilted just slightly forward, and he kept slipping down it. He wanted to change to another, but he saw that the others all had the same problem. He clenched the muscles in his thighs and tried to forget this annoyance, immersing himself in the leaflets and booklets on the table.

They were all completely heterogeneous, in truth: a few press clippings on The Firm sat alongside the canteen menus for the last two months of the previous year, and an organogram, which was made entirely illegible by the poor quality of its photocopying, lay next to the assessment of a visit to an Asian industrialist who specialised in the production of soy sauce. There was also a volume that was supposed to comprise, as its title said, the complete List of The Firm's members of staff from 1 January of the current year, arranged by country, position and sector, but all this contained was two or three hundred blank sheets. The Investigator also found sign-up forms for a tango evening organised by the Association of Technical Executives of the Region 3 Transportation Services, a circular notifying the warehousemen of the International Packaging Sector of the opening of a rest home in the Balkans, the instruction manual in ten languages for a German-brand Dictaphone, an invoice for the purchase of thirty litres of liquid soap, as well as two dozen photographs showing a building under construction whose exact location and intended purpose were not specified.

The Investigator went conscientiously through each of these documents, telling himself that he might be able to understand the logic that had brought them all together. But it all remained quite unclear. It nonetheless took him half an hour to read through and scrutinise them, and the Guide still had not come back down the stairs.

Suddenly the Investigator brought his hand to his belly. A long gurgling had just shaken his guts. It was no wonder. He had not swallowed a thing since the two dreadful rusks that morning, and the previous evening he had not eaten anything at all. A bit further on, behind the first turn of the staircase, he saw what looked like a drinks vending machine. He had two coins left. Perhaps he could find something there to settle his hunger? He got up, and discovered that his muscles were completely in spasm because of these wretched chairs.

Bent double, his thighs tense and taut, he hobbled over to the machine, twice almost falling as he trod on the hem of his overall that trailed on the floor. But the sight behind the glass was enough to make him forget his pains: it offered a large selection of hot and cold drinks, but mainly, and he had not been expecting this at all, dozens of sandwiches – chicken, ham, sausage, tuna, garnished with green salad, sliced tomatoes and mayonnaise, wonderfully fresh, waiting behind the refrigerated glass, each carefully wrapped in cellophane.

## 17

HIS CHOICE LIGHTED ON A HOT CHOCOLATE AND A "RUSTICA": "A hearty cut of traditional ham off the bone, between two slices of home-baked bread spread with lightly salted butter, lettuce leaves, gherkins, thinly sliced tomatoes," read the description.

Number 7 for the chocolate, and number 32 for the Rustica. The Investigator put his coins in, typed the numbers, activated the control button, which began to blink. The machine started to speak: "Your order is being processed. Number 7. Hot chocolate. If you would like more sugar, press the button marked 'Sugar'."

It was a synthesised, mechanical voice, vaguely feminine, pleasant to listen to in spite of the strong foreign accent that he couldn't place. From within the machine came sucking noises, valves opening and closing, suction and expulsion, then a little door slid open on the right, revealing the spout of a kind of percolator, steam coming out of it, followed quickly by the smooth, boiling jet of chocolate, smelling delicious, creamy, frothy, that before the dismayed Investigator's eyes flowed right out as no cup had first been presented to receive the beverage. When the flow stopped, the artificial voice told the Investigator she hoped he'd enjoy it, and it was only once she had finished talking that the white plastic cup, with a short, ironic "plop!", took its position to receive the lost drink. The Investigator did not have time to get annoyed or to give in to despair, as the delivery of Number 32 was about to take place.

"You have requested a Rustica sandwich. Please collect it from the compartment at the bottom of the machine. We wish you a *bon appétit*."

The revolving stand on which the sandwiches were held began to move. It turned three times to position Number 32 right in front of a remote-controlled arm which grabbed hold of it, removed it from its section, carried it some thirty centimetres through the air and then opened its four claws to drop it: the Rustica dropped towards the delivery compartment, but about twenty centimetres before reaching it, it lodged in the range of Number 65s, the "Ocean" sandwiches: "A tasty tuna steak nestling in a sesame roll with olive oil, endive salad, onions and capers."

The Investigator tried his best to slap the palm of his hand against the machine's glass, but the Rustica did not want to leave the Oceans. He hit it harder and harder, grabbed hold of the machine, shook it in every direction, and all he managed to achieve was a repeat of the synthesised voice congratulating him on the completion of his order, reminding him that he was about to enjoy a meal designed according to the strictest sanitary and dietary standards in accordance with international Conventions, and wishing him a very *bon appétit*.

He dropped to the ground, put his arm into the delivery

compartment, contorted himself, shoved back the helmet that was getting in the way of his manoeuvring, reached out his hand and his fingers, as far as he could, but alas, despite all his efforts, his helpless middle finger was still a good ten centimetres from the sandwich.

"You should have asked me!"

The Investigator quickly pulled his arm out of the machine, like a thief surprised by the police with his fingers in an old lady's handbag.

The Guide was looking at him, shaking his head.

"I would have told you it was not working. We keep calling the company that looks after it, but it's impossible to make ourselves understood. They've relocated their production unit to Bangladesh, and nobody here yet speaks Bengali. We have no trouble getting them on the phone, but after that communication becomes impossible. Don't make that face, you're not the first, we've all fallen for it. It's a shame, too, because when it works it really is very good. Shall we go? The Manager is waiting for you."

The Guide was already walking towards the staircase. The Investigator got up as quickly as he could, tugged at his overall, repositioned his helmet, which was about to fall off, and followed him. The gurglings in his belly were growing. He really did need to eat something otherwise he was afraid he might pass out. The beginning of the climb was quite a struggle, his feet kept getting tangled in the hem of the overall. He had to take hold of it with his two hands and hitch it up a few inches like a bride with the cascading tulle of the train on her wedding dress. He felt utterly ridiculous.

"Have you had time to glance over the paperwork?" asked the Guide.

The Investigator nodded.

"Informative, isn't it? I wasn't the one who prepared the file for you, I only supervised the procedure. They assigned me a Colleague from our Temporary Processing Division, who've had their personnel cut. He was the one who really took on the work. Shame I can't keep him, they're sending him to the Conceptualisation Department. An incomparable Colleague – brilliant, subtle, committed, with an extraordinary gift for synthesis, perfectly representative of the culture of The Firm. We need more like him."

The Investigator thought it was best not to reply. And reply to what? Apparently the Guide hadn't been looking at the same documents, the ones he was referring to must have been swapped with the ones they'd given him, which must originally have been meant for a rubbish bin or a shredder.

The helicoid shape made by the staircase was exceedingly harmonious. Probably of no use in terms of efficiency, it gave the person using it a peculiar feeling of lightness as he rose, free of any breaks, corners, anything that might be pointed, aggressive, apt to cause injury. The higher you climbed, the closer you came to the central axis as the distance of the staircase's steps from this axis decreased, which meant that eventually the Investigator started feeling as though he were just turning round and round on himself without going any further up, which increased his sense of vertigo and for a time made him forget his hunger.

"Here we are," the Guide said.

The two men were standing at a large door made out of precious wood, with no handle anywhere to be seen.

"Knock, the Manager is expecting you. As for me, my task is now done. I don't expect we'll see each other again. So I hope the rest of your day goes well. I shall not shake your hand."

The Guide bowed to the Investigator, who in turn felt himself obliged, so as not to appear impolite, to do the same. The Guide moved away along a narrow, curving corridor that swallowed him up in seconds.

The Investigator checked that his overall was correctly buttoned, that his badge was on straight. He repositioned his helmet, which had a tendency to keep slipping, then knocked on the door, three short knocks. As if by magic, it opened in absolute silence. He was met by a violent light, a projector, perhaps, pointed towards him, blinding him. He blinked, shielded his eyes with his right hand, and heard a loud voice call out to him:

"Come in! Do come in! Step forward! Come now, do step forward! Don't be afraid!"

# 18

YET AGAIN, ONE MORE TIME, THE INVESTIGATOR THOUGHT ABOUT death. Hadn't he sometimes read the accounts of that liminal experience that some people go through, when they return from the frontiers of the beyond, and how they talk of an intense radiant light, a sort of tunnel through which they'd moved forward before returning back? The glass cone he'd entered, the curious staircase that wound in on itself, this great sun that poured each of its particles into his eyes, flooding them, weren't these all variations on that great tunnel?

"Please, don't just stand there! Come! Oh, do come on!"

The voice was loud, slightly derisive. The Investigator thought that God, if he really did exist, surely didn't have such a voice, which rather reminded him of that of a used-car salesman or a politician.

"And what are you doing with that helmet? You poor old thing! Who told you to wear that grotesque helmet? You aren't in a shipyard! Come in! Do come in!"

No, this quite decidedly could not be God. God wouldn't have made a comment about the safety helmet. And if it wasn't God, then that meant he wasn't dead. In which case the light was just a bright light, with nothing divine about it at all. But in that case why the hell was it still trained on him?

"The thing is, I can't see anything . . ."

"What do you mean you can't see anything? I can see you perfectly! Perfectly!"

"I'm being blinded!" the Investigator groaned.

"Blinded? Damn!" the voice said. "But of course! Who put this wretched . . . Wait!"

The Investigator heard a sharp little click, then was plunged into total darkness.

"There, is that better?" the voice said.

"I can't see anything now, I can't see anything at all," the Investigator moaned.

"But that's not possible! I can still see you! This whole business is crazy! Close your eyes for a few seconds, and then open them back up slowly and I'm sure you'll be able to see me. Go on! Trust me! I'm telling you, close your eyes!"

The Investigator resigned himself to doing what he was told. He didn't have much to lose. After all, if he was dead, he couldn't be more so, death being a state, he thought, which didn't allow for superlatives. One cannot be very dead, or exceptionally dead. You're just dead, full stop, that's it.

He reopened his eyes to find the room he'd just entered. He immediately thought of the office of a film producer. He'd never seen one, but he had a very precise and also quite imaginary idea of what they were like: expensive wood fittings, a bookcase holding awards and trophies, a bar on castors, a cigar box, a huge photograph on the wall depicting an old man who looked like the one on the key-ring, a thick carpet, leather armchairs, a desk with a large rosewood tray holding a paper knife, a luxury pen, a blotter, a letter-rack, a heavy inkwell, a pencil pot.

"At last, now can you see me?"

The Investigator nodded, but the truth was he couldn't really see all that much, only a dense figure half-sitting on the left-hand side of the desk.

"But for goodness' sake, do remove that helmet – please! Who kitted you out in a helmet like that?"

"Someone told me it was compulsory."

"Compulsory? Who was this 'someone'? We don't have 'some-ones' here. I want a name. Who? And that overall? I'm impressed at how docile you are."

"I'd rather keep the overall on, if it's all the same to you," the Investigator replied, not wanting to inform on the Guide about the helmet, and remembering the dreadful state of the clothes he was wearing under the overall.

"As you wish! Come on in, make yourself comfortable."

The Investigator took off the helmet and walked towards the desk. The figure became clearer as he got up. It was a man on the smallish side, decidedly bald, and whose slightly round features were barely revealed by a light that came down from the ceiling like a shower of golden grain.

"Sit down, sit down . . ."

The man gestured him towards one of the two armchairs. The Investigator sat down. He felt as though he'd shrunk as he lost himself completely in the armchair which was of an uncommon size. He pulled the fabric of his overall down onto his legs in order to hide his trousers and put the helmet down on his lap.

"First things first," continued the man, who must have been the Manager the Guide had told him about, "I'd like you to feel quite comfortable, to make yourself at home. Just as though you were in your own home. Alright?"

"Alright."

"You were saying just now that you were blinded?"

"That's because of your light, I couldn't see anything. It was a figure of speech."

The Manager clapped his hands and got up.

"Excuse me, you're talking to me about figures of speech, I don't want figures of speech, I want facts, and clear-sightedness, I'm really counting on you, and when I say I, what I really mean is we. You understand?"

"Of course," replied the Investigator, who didn't understand much and who was feeling as though he was being gradually digested by the armchair.

"At last! Are you alright? You look very pale . . ."

The Investigator hesitated, and then, as he was feeling weaker and weaker, he steeled himself and took the plunge.

"The thing is, you see, I haven't eaten anything in a long time, if it might perhaps be possible to get something—"

"Possible? You're joking! Naturally it's possible! Need I remind you who you are? Are you not . . ." The Manager hesitated, rummaged in his pockets, drew out a set of index cards that he consulted quickly. "Are you not . . . now let me see . . . you are . . . you are . . . oh, damn, where did I put your card!"

"I'm the Investigator."

"Right! Thank you. That's it, you're the Investigator! Are you really the Investigator?"

"Yes."

"Do you really believe that in a firm like ours we wouldn't set everything in motion for your Investigation to unfold in the best possible conditions?"

"That would indeed be most kind of you . . ."

"Well, then!"

And he began to laugh, as he picked up the telephone.

"This is the Manager. Bring us something for the Investigator to eat as quickly as possible."

He stopped talking, seemed to be listening alertly to what someone was saying on the other end of the line, shook his head several times, covered the receiver up with his hand suddenly and said to the Investigator:

"Chicken liver salad, roast beef, green beans, goat's cheese, chocolate fondant, it's not much, I'm afraid, but would that do you?"

"But that's . . . wonderful," the Investigator managed to mumble, unable to believe his ears.

"And to drink? Red wine, white wine, beer, raki, ouzo, grappa, pisco, tokay, spirytus, aqua vitae, bourbon, mineral water, sparkling, still, originating from where? Fiji? Iceland? Italy? Guatemala?"

"Perhaps something hot," ventured the Investigator who was shivering with cold, "ideally a tea . . ."

"A tea? Japanese, Taiwanese, Russian, Ceylon, Darjeeling, white, black, green, red, blue?"

"Tea, just . . . as it comes," the Investigator ventured.

"As it comes? No problem!" replied the Manager, who passed on the order and hung up. "And that's it! You see, you needn't have worried! The Firm's kitchens, like The Firm itself, too, never stop. They operate every hour of the day and night, every day of the year."

"But . . . aren't we still in daytime . . . ?" asked the Investigator, doubtful.

"Of course we're in daytime! Look at that light," said the Manager, gesturing towards the large picture windows. "'We're in daytime' . . . That's a strange expression when you think about it, *we're in daytime*, don't you think? By the way, in the interests of honesty I ought to tell you that the beef comes from the southern hemisphere, you don't have any problem with that?"

"What beef?"

"From the roast, of course, the dish I've just ordered for you!"

The Investigator smiled faintly.

"Well then," the Manager went on. "Now there's nothing to do but wait."

He crossed his arms across his belly and looked at the Investigator benevolently. The Investigator gave him an exaggerated smile and sank a little further into the armchair. His head now reached just above the armrests. The Manager gave a sigh, and the two men waited.

# 19

THEY REALLY DID WAIT A LONG TIME. IN SILENCE, AT FIRST. THEN, because silence and smiles can only go so far, the Manager, who had come to sit beside the Investigator, in the other armchair, struck up conversation, reassuring his guest that the arrival of the food was imminent.

"We're going through difficult times, you're well aware of that. Very difficult. Who can say what will become of us, of you, me, the planet . . . ? Nothing's simple. A little water? No? As you wish. After all, if you don't mind, I can confide in you, it's lonely in this job, terribly lonely, and you're a sort of doctor, aren't you?"

"Not really," murmured the Investigator.

"Come now, don't be so modest!" said the Manager, patting him on the thigh. Then he breathed in slowly, closed his eyes, breathed out, opened his eyes again.

"Remind me of the exact purpose of your visit?"

"It's not exactly a visit, really. I've got to investigate the suicides that have affected The Firm."

"Suicides? First I've heard of it . . . They must have kept it from me. My colleagues know not to upset me. Suicides – just think! – if

I'd been kept informed, God only knows what I might have been able to do! Suicides . . ."

The Manager thought about the word dreamily, a discreet smile blooming on his face, as though he were toying with a pleasant idea.

"Suicide – I'd never thought about it before, but deep down, yes, why not, it's no more stupid than anything else . . . You know," he went on, the smile now consigned to oblivion, "I devote my time to just one thing: trying to understand why we've got to where we are. I imagine that's what's expected of me, but I haven't got anywhere. No conclusions. Completely counterproductive. Is there one person, someone, anywhere, who can understand it? I don't know what your view is personally?"

The Investigator was quite troubled by the shape this interview was beginning to take. He shrugged, slowly, which could have been interpreted as a prolonging of the Manager's questioning or an expression of metaphysical doubt.

"Of course," said the Manager. "Of course. You are a wise man, you operate on a higher plain. But I'm not like you, alas, I'm not like you, I get my hands dirty! I'm a simple pawn, a sort of mite. Have you read the philosophers? Of course you've read them, a man like you has read them. Just imagine, they put me in a state of intellectual catalepsy. It's wild. And they must know it, the bastards! No doubt they've done it on purpose. Deep down those people are terribly cruel, and the most incredible cowards."

As he spoke, the Manager was twisting his fingers as if he wanted to pull them out.

"Damn it, if only you knew what my days are like, between you and me, I can tell you, my days, I spend them . . . questioning myself. Yes, I question myself. I don't leave this office. That's all I do. Under the gaze of . . ."

He stopped, coughed, and it seemed to the Investigator that he'd turned towards the large photograph showing the easy-going, smiling old man whose bushy white eyebrows elegantly matched the large, slightly drooping bow tie knotted round the collar of his shirt. He nodded his head and turned back to the Investigator.

"Yes, I question myself," the Manager went on. "What has become of our ideals? We've trampled them, plundered them. I'm not talking about you, I wouldn't presume, you're different, you're above us, but me, I'm as despicable as a rat dropping, a centipede, an old cigarette butt that's soggy and coming apart, squashed by the heel of an anonymous, contemptuous shoe, I really am, I am, don't say I'm not just to make me happy. For pity's sake, don't try to spare me! You should be implacable – just, but implacable! And why so, why? I'm asking you, I'm asking you, since you're someone who knows, since you, you do know, don't you? Don't you know?"

The Investigator didn't dare disappoint the Manager and nodded slightly.

"But of course you know . . . Oh, it's just all so . . . But I'm rambling!"

He clapped his hands, got up nimbly, executed a little dance step, almost falling as he caught his feet in the thick carpet.

"Look at me! I've got some resources left, all the same, haven't

I? I'm not yet finished in spite of my age! What do you think?"

The Investigator was getting weaker. The armchair was turning into a large mouth that was progressively swallowing him, and this man in front of him, who was jumping up and down like a sportsman warming up, struck him as even more worrying than the Policeman at the Hotel.

The Manager began to do leaps, springs, pike-jumps. He spun around, then ran to the end of the room, crossed himself, took his run-up, charged towards his large desk onto which he tried to jump, and almost succeeded, but at the last moment, when he was hanging in the air, his left foot caught the huge black marble inkwell and he crashed heavily against the glass wall.

The Investigator was about to come to his help but the Manager was already back on his feet. Smiling, he massaged his elbow and knee as he kept repeating: "I'm fine, absolutely fine. I'm used to it. Used to it . . . You will tell them, won't you? You will tell them I'm at the peak of my abilities? That I can still, oh, I don't know, I can hang on, hang on, yes, hang on!!!! I'm right here. I'm right here! You'll tell them? Please? Please . . ."

The Manager had kneeled down in front of the Investigator. His hands were clasped. His eyes were flooded with tears. He was begging.

"Of course," said the Investigator, "I'll tell them. I'll tell them, don't worry yourself about it." And as he was saying those words that seemed to be coming from someone else, he was wondering how to get out of this situation.

"Sometimes, at night, I feel like I'm the captain of a huge airliner." The Manager's voice had shrunk to a murmur. "I am responsible for five hundred passengers, or five thousand, or five hundred thousand, I don't know anymore, I'm holding the controls . . ."

Still on his knees, he was clutching the Investigator's legs. For a few seconds his mouth imitated the noise of the jet engines.

"I'm this great pilot. People are sleeping, reading, dreaming about their loves, building their futures with sweet, tender fantasies, and me – as for me, it all comes down to me, God has touched His index finger to my brow, I know the way, I know the skies, the stars, the currents and the souls, I have that great dashboard before me, all lit up, those magnificent buttons, white, opal, yellow, reddish, orange, silvery, all those lives that light up, go off, blink, those joysticks, so nice to the touch, what intoxication to feel there behind me, shut up in the same aluminium cabin, the destinies of all those beings, but I'm only a man, a man, damn it, why me? So why should I be the captain? Why me? I don't have any skill! None at all! I don't know how to read a chart, I have no sense of direction and I've never been able to get the smallest little kite up into the air! It's a horrible dream."

There was a silence. The Manager had begun to cry and his tears were making the Investigator's trousers wet. As for him, troubled by this turn of events, he didn't dare say a thing. He was considering what to do when the Manager leapt back to his feet, rubbed his face with his hands, banished his tears, and turned to the Investigator with a face smoothed into an enormous smile.

"Life really is magnificent, don't you agree?"

The Investigator didn't reply. He had just seen a man disintegrate beneath his eyes like a used-up old battery unable to retain its charge, and then all of a sudden this same man – but was this really the same man? – was rejoicing at existence, having wiped the tears from his face with the back of his hand. The Investigator didn't have time to reply.

"If you'll excuse me? I'll just be a second. I'll be right back."

The Manager pointed towards a door to the left of his huge desk.

"Please," said the Investigator. The Manager clapped his hands, performed an elegant leap and danced towards the door in a bossa nova rhythm, and then, having reached it, he turned, gave a gracious gesture as though greeting an imaginary audience, opened the door, and disappeared, closing it behind him.

## 20

HUNGER IS A CURIOUS CONTINENT. THE INVESTIGATOR HAD NEVER thought of it as a country before now, but he was beginning to see it like that, stretched out, vast and desolate. He felt his head hum and it seemed as though the walls of the room were swaying slightly. The beneficial effects of the two tablets that the Policeman had given him had disappeared long ago. He had to resign himself to the evidence: he had a raging fever. He was shivering in spite of the heat in the room and the thick overall keeping him warm. His mouth was dry and he had the unpleasant feeling that his tongue would stick to his palate for good. His hollow belly was giving off strange noises, like complaints, echoes of distant arguments, muffled collisions, faint explosions. From time to time his vision clouded over. His heart was beating strangely, alternating between quick accelerations and worrying pauses. He tried to reassure himself a little, telling himself that the Manager had doubtless gone to enquire after the meal he had ordered, that in a few minutes he would be back with the dish he had offered him and that all this would stop.

The Manager . . . Was this town home to no-one but strange

figures like the Giantess or totally unhinged ones like the Policeman or this man? All his incomprehensible moaning had truly stunned him, and though the Investigator was not totally stupid he had not been able to understand much. Where had he come from? And why such a need to open himself up like that to the first stranger he came across? He didn't know him from Adam, after all! Had he no self-restraint, no modesty? How did this depressive individual come to hold such an important position, when you didn't need to be a psychologist to conclude from all the evidence that he had neither the mental substance nor the robust nerves to take on this kind of responsibility? And then that gigantic portrait which he had looked at several times with both fear and admiration, as if seeking support, or even authorisation, who did it represent who immediately instilled in him both veneration and fear?

The Investigator looked at it more closely. The old man's smile was direct, deep and candid. It was not a manufactured smile, but the smile of someone who loves his fellow man, knows him and contemplates him with benevolence and humanity. The old man was dressed in a well-cut suit, a little outdated, perhaps, but which looked just right on him, made of a supple, warm, reassuring material, no doubt a tweed. He was leaning forward, as though to come as close as possible to the person looking at him.

This was surely the Founder, the Investigator said to himself. The Founder of The Firm. Who else could he be? For all that, he had no recollection at all of The Firm having had a Founder. Even if it had, of course, been created at some moment or other, and indubitably by one individual or other. The scant documentation that his Head of Department had given him when he'd taken charge of the Investigation made no such reference, restricted as it was to the counting out of the recorded suicides, and the file that the Guide had handed him a little earlier, that afternoon, incoherent as it was, didn't contain anything on the subject either.

Ordinarily the Investigator wouldn't be concerned with the origins of firms, their civil status, so to speak. That wasn't his business. And besides, in the world he lived in, they had become sort of nebulous, adding subsidiaries to themselves like so many particles, relocating, re-relocating, creating ramifications, distant tree-like structures, rootlets, interweaving their stake-holdings, the staff and the boards of directors up in such confusing tangles that you could no longer quite tell who was who and who did what. In such conditions, getting back to their foundations required an economic archaeology that far surpassed the Investigator's competences and curiosity. He even wondered why such questions were crossing his mind at all. He really wasn't his usual self. No doubt his fever was rising. The huge old man in the portrait was still looking at him, but his smile seemed to have changed: from having been benevolent, it was now proving to be rather more ironic.

Suddenly his eyelids felt terribly heavy and he closed them for a fraction of a second, but then, when he reopened them, he saw that the office had been plunged into gloom. The lightness that a few moments earlier had been coming in from outside through the two large picture-windows had in an instant been replaced by deep, black, utterly dark night. And all this in the blink of an eye! He got up out of the armchair, panic-stricken, and rushed over towards the windows. Yes, it really was night. But how long had he closed his eyes for, then? Could he really have fallen asleep for a good length of time? And if that was the case, what had happened to the Manager? What time was it? He consulted his watch: the hands were showing 9.43 p.m. He went over to the door through which his host had disappeared. He knocked three times, then four, then five, louder and louder. No-one answered. He flattened his ear up against the panelling. Nothing, not even the tiniest sound. He put his hand on the doorknob, turned it. The door was locked. He shook the doorknob more and more desperately.

"Might I know what you're doing in this office at this hour?"

The Investigator froze. He felt his blood congeal in his veins. There was someone standing behind him, a few metres away. Someone who had come into the room without his hearing.

"Put your hands slowly in the air, and turn around without making any sudden movements," the voice went on, and it was far from friendly.

## 21

THE INVESTIGATOR SPUN AROUND, WHILE LIFTING HIS ARMS HIGH, his hands open, palms spread, to prove he was not carrying a weapon.

"That's it, just like that, very good," continued the voice, which he seemed to recognise. "Now, don't move."

The man levelled a torch at the Investigator, its beam sweeping over him from head to toe.

"I'm going to switch on the light. But pay attention, you're still not to move. I'm armed, and at the slightest movement you're done for. Understand?"

The Investigator, whose eyes had ended up getting used to the gloom, suddenly felt like a laboratory rat being observed under a spotlight. He blinked, and after a moment managed to make out the man who was aiming at him.

"Hang on – it's you?" said the Investigator at last, reassured, recognising the Guide and starting to drop his arms.

"DON'T MOVE! You are to keep your hands up!" said the other man in a hard, dry voice. "I won't hesitate to shoot."

Yet the Investigator couldn't have been mistaken. It really was the Guide, it was the man who had led him into this same office, a few hours earlier. It couldn't be anyone else, unless he had a perfect clone. Only his clothes had changed: he was no longer wearing an elegant grey double-breasted suit but a black one-piece jumpsuit zipped up the front, cinched at the waist with a linen belt, a cap in the same colour and knee-length military boots. His right hand was holding an impressively large revolver.

"But come now, please," the Investigator babbled, "we know one another! You're the—"

"NOT ANOTHER WORD OR I SHALL FEEL COMPELLED TO USE MY WEAPON!" yelled the man, approaching him quickly, keeping him constantly lined up in his sights. When he was within reach of the Investigator, he pinned him up against the wall, forced his two arms behind his back, handcuffed him with the help of a set of plastic straps and then pushed him unceremoniously towards the exit, having first taken the trouble to cover his head with the helmet which had been left on one of the armchairs.

All this happened in less than thirty seconds, and the Investigator hadn't had the chance to react or to say a word. The man's revolver didn't seem to be a toy, and in any case he felt far too weak to try anything. Before they left the room, the man with the gun looked at the large photograph of the old man, and as though speaking to him more than to the Investigator, he declaimed in a loud voice:

"THE POLICE HAVE BEEN NOTIFIED, THEY WILL BE HERE ANY MINUTE NOW, AND THEN YOU WILL HAVE TO ANSWER FOR YOUR ACTIONS."

Then he hurried him into the corridor, launched himself out, too, and closed the door sharply behind them.

"Good Lord . . .!"

The man was breathing heavily, and he laughed a bit nervously, looked at the Investigator and sliced open the cuffs with the help of a knife.

"Sorry about that, but I had to play the game; I'm convinced that room is crammed full of mics, and cameras, too, no doubt."

The Investigator no longer understood a thing.

"I really thought you were going to give me away . . ."

"So you are the one who . . . You *are* the Guide?"

Suddenly the man looked annoyed.

"Absolutely not. After a certain time I become the Watchman . . . You understand, my salary is so poor . . . I've set things up so that if I get into the IT system I can combine the two posts, but if anyone from Central Management finds out, I'm done for . . . You won't tell anyone, will you? I'm sure you can grasp that a man in my position would be prepared to do anything. A desperate man has nothing to lose."

While he said this, he had waved his weapon in front of the Investigator's eyes. The Investigator answered with a look that he would keep the secret.

"I don't have any other way out. It's humiliating, but what do you expect, when you're not cut out to be a leader you've no choice but to increase the number of walk-on parts you play to get by . . . No, please keep your helmet on!"

The Investigator repositioned the headgear, having given up on trying to understand why one person insisted on his wearing it while another told him to remove it at once.

"So it's you, then – damn! What were you still doing in the office at this hour?"

Without going into details, the Investigator had to recount what the Manager had said, but he passed silently over the attempted leap onto the desk and the pathetic position into which he had subsequently put himself, kneeling in tears at his feet. Then he explained how the Manager had left quickly, which he had put down to courtesy: what else could he have been doing but going to check up on the food he'd ordered and which hadn't yet shown up?

"But what are you saying? The Firm's restaurant has been closed for works for fourteen months! The Manager is perfectly aware of that. It's created plenty of turmoil among the staff, there's even been threat of a strike! How could he have promised you such a thing? Are you sure you understood him correctly?"

The Investigator wasn't sure of anything at all anymore. Not even of his own name. He shrugged, resigned.

"In any case, it's been ages since the Manager left The Firm. I personally saw him leave the tower at the end of the afternoon. Come on now, you can't stay here, if anyone finds you it's bound to end up on my head."

The Guide who was now the Watchman put his weapon back in its holster, gave the Investigator a little pat on the shoulder and gestured for him to follow. They took the same staircase the two of them had come up some hours earlier. But just as the first time the Investigator had felt a pleasant light-headedness as he climbed, on the way down he was gripped by a nausea that engulfed him and made all the aluminium and steel structures of the tower seem soft as marshmallows. The corners blended into curves, the straight lines mutated into moving snakes, the steps themselves became mobile, rubbery, incomparably treacherous, as springy as a carpet of moss. The world was coming apart as he made his way down, rather as though someone were dismantling a stage set that was past its usefulness, and he knew he ought not to dawdle as he surely risked being absorbed by this fleeting, yielding, moving substance, as easily as used water can be swallowed up into a gutter.

## 22

A TERRIFIC SLAP BROUGHT HIM BACK TO CONSCIOUSNESS.

"I'm sorry about that, I wasn't sure what else I could do. You just let yourself slide into my arms at the bottom of the stairs, I had to drag you outside, and once we were out no sooner had the door closed than you fell like a ripe fruit! Do you feel better?"

The Night Watchman was standing beside the Investigator who was curled up on the ground. His concerned face did not show any trace of compassion and there was nothing friendly about his question. The Investigator sketched a vague gesture with his hand to make the man understand there was nothing to worry about.

"At least you aren't carrying any viruses?" the Watchman continued. "Because The Firm really doesn't need an epidemic right now."

"You needn't be afraid," the Investigator managed to murmur. "It's just . . . I haven't eaten anything substantial since yesterday morning . . ."

The Watchman seemed surprised:

"Since yesterday morning, you say . . . ?"

He stopped to think.

"That's only two days. You mustn't have a very solid constitution to be in this state after only two little days of fasting, that or you don't have the willpower. Six months ago, the Deputy Head of Export Services went on a hunger strike. He refused to let them send him off on early retirement. Guess how many days he held out?"

The Investigator shook his head to mean he had no idea.

"No, no, say a number!"

"Fifteen days . . . ?"

"Forty-two! He held out for forty-two days! Can you believe it? Forty-two days! The Management didn't want to give in. And they were right! THEY WERE ABSOLUTELY RIGHT NOT TO GIVE IN!"

He had yelled this phrase, while looking about him. Then he fell silent, calmed down and turned back to the Investigator who was still on the ground and who was beginning to feel the beneficial effects of the fresh air.

"How did it end?"

"Sorry?"

"You were telling me about a hunger strike . . . ?"

"Ah yes," said the Watchman, as though setting foot back on a shore he'd left some time ago, "the D.H.E.S.? He died. That was all. The body has its limits. Forty-two days, that's a lot. Too much. Some people never know when to stop. As a result, no early retirement, no retirement at all. Nothing. One less grumbler, one place that's freed up and that makes some other person happy."

"I wasn't told about that case," moaned the Investigator. "At least, I don't think I was, it wasn't referred to in any of the documents that—"

He was interrupted abruptly by the Watchman.

"And why should anyone have notified you of the Deputy Head of Export Services dying from a hunger strike? Why? Aren't you here to investigate the suicides? And only the suicides?"

"Indeed," the Investigator explained, "if you think about it, that sort of behaviour might resemble a kind of suicide . . ."

The Watchman parted his legs slightly, crossed his arms over his belly, pushed his cap back up, and remained quiet for a few seconds, apparently in thought. Above him the sky was as black as his uniform, so it looked to the Investigator as though only his eyes were emerging from the darkness, large, wide, furious eyes. Eventually the Watchman uncrossed his arms and pointed his right index finger at the Investigator threateningly:

"So tell me, you who've not eaten for two days, according to what you've just told me, if I follow your reasoning, wouldn't that make you someone in the process of trying to commit suicide?"

Snow covered the ground, not very thick, delicate and perfectly pure. The Investigator had only just noticed it. In the sky there was nothing but blackness, and on the ground this big white carpet on which, what was more, his buttocks were resting. The wind battered the overall that he was still wearing carefully buttoned up and which kept him pleasantly warm. The helmet was protecting his bald skull. It was freezing, he was sure of that, and yet he wasn't cold, he wasn't cold at all. He even felt as though he were going numb in a warmth that was smooth and rich. He could have fallen asleep there, by that entry door, yes, he could have slept for hours, to escape from this situation that refused to make any sense.

The Watchman was waiting, his left fist on his hip, his right hand on the grip of his revolver.

"I'm hungry," the Investigator said at last. "I'd eat anything without making a fuss. I swear it . . ."

At once the Watchman relaxed, exhaled hard, let go of his gun, and wiped his forehead.

"Good Lord, you really frightened me there! You only just got away with that! Yes, you just saved your life. I was a heartbeat away from thinking you were a mole!"

"A mole?"

"Yes, that you'd been turned, if you'd rather I put it like that, it happens all the time in espionage."

"But I'm not a spy, I'm the Inv—"

"I know perfectly well who you are, but I do know what I'm trying to say. Think about it: someone is sent to investigate a wave of suicides, but he turns out to be a dangerous suicide himself and so everything is distorted, the system is sabotaged, everything explodes, it's all over! Now do you get it?"

"Not really . . ." murmured the Investigator, who could no longer feel his hands sunk into the snow.

"It's not important. Get back on your feet, damn it! You've got to leave now, you'll come back tomorrow."

The Watchman grabbed hold of him and pulled him up, leaned him up against the wall and then rifled through the pockets of his own uniform. At last he found what he had been looking for and held it out to the Investigator.

"Here, it's all I've got."

The Investigator took a kind of large, brown, wrinkled stone, ten centimetres long, more or less circular in cross-section, and which was slightly hollowed out in the middle. He looked up at the Watchman, not daring to formulate his question, but the other man pre-empted him.

"Top quality. It might be a little dry, I must have forgotten it in my overalls for three months, but it's meant well."

And as the Investigator was hesitating at the thing he was holding in his hand, the Watchman's expression turned icy again and he went on, suspiciously:

"Now don't tell me that on top of everything else you don't eat pork?"

# 23

WHEN THE INVESTIGATOR WAS AT LAST ON THE PAVEMENT, trembling with fear, he turned back to take one last look at the Guard, but the man had already gone back to reading the sports page of his newspaper and chewing the last of his sandwich.

After he had given him the sausage, the Watchman had scarcely addressed another word to him, settling for guiding him mechanically in the right direction, since it was impossible to make out the red, green or yellow lines on the ground now that they had been covered by snow. Once close to the Guardhouse, the Watchman had made him stop and ordered him to remove the overall, the helmet and the badge.

"They will be returned to you tomorrow. Firm property must not leave The Firm."

The Investigator put his hands in the pockets of the overall, took out the key-ring with the portrait of the old man and made as if to return it to the Watchman.

"No, keep it, it'll bring you luck!"

The Investigator reluctantly handed over the thick overall and the too-small helmet. It was rather as if he had suddenly found himself naked, naked and frozen, his raincoat and his suit being far too thin and still too damp to protect him from the more and more bitter cold.

"Yesterday evening the Guard asked me if I was the bearer of Exceptional Authorisation – would it be possible for me to get that, it might be useful for me to have . . ."

The Investigator had hunched over a little. He was expecting a denial, a scandalised response, perhaps some kind of lecture, an unlikely or delirious explanation from the Watchman, but the man did not say a word. He took a pen from the top pocket of his overalls and a sort of square piece of card from his trouser pocket and scribbled something, then gave the document to the Investigator.

"Here. I don't know what use Exceptional Authorisation might be to you, but there you are. And now I'll ask you to excuse me, I've got work to do."

He turned on his heel and strode away, disappearing into the shadows and the whirlwinds of snow. The Investigator looked at what the Watchman had given him: it was a beermat advertising a brand of beer, stained and dog-eared, on which he had written "Exceptional Authorisation granted to the bearer of this card".

The Investigator almost called him back, but he didn't have the strength. After all, the beermat was of a piece with everything else. What else should he have expected? He set about approaching the Guardhouse where he could see a light on, and under that light, the lowered head of a man.

The path he had to follow to get there was a long one, even

though the distance in a straight line cannot have been more than twenty metres, but the portcullises, the rolls of barbed wire, the chicanes, the chevaux-de-frises that had been positioned around there dictated a labyrinthine route that prevented both intrusions and hurried exits. The Investigator saw that the Guard had noticed him, and was now observing his progress. He thought he ought to give him a wave, with a smile, to get into his good books, but as he did so, he flicked the right side of his raincoat, the one with the pocket hanging off, and the fabric caught on the steel teeth of a piece of barbed wire and, without a qualm, it ripped a tear in it that was a good thirty centimetres across. Such matter is admirable, it knows no feeling, and its existence is never burdened with any weakness. You can put it anywhere and it does its job. Only the elements, over the course of millennia, trouble it, but it knows nothing about that. Despite this incident, the Investigator kept his smile, in order not to draw the guard's attention to the fact that if he studied him too closely he would very soon notice he looked like a tramp.

"Good evening!"

The Investigator had summoned all his remaining energy to pronounce those two simple words in a natural way. The Guard was spreading the contents of a tin of pâté onto half a baguette. He was a slightly round-faced man, almost bald. In front of him, a newspaper open on the page with the sports results was dotted with breadcrumbs. A half-empty bottle of wine stood beside an ashtray in which a cigarette lay smoking. Above the Guard's head, a little to his left, the control monitors showed still images of different exterior and interior parts of The Firm. No human being appeared in any of them. From these fragmented portraits of the place a troubling impression of unreality emerged, as though someone had trained surveillance cameras on movie sets that were now abandoned, or which perhaps had never been used at all.

The Guard had looked up and pressed the button on his microphone.

"Good evening! Not too warm out, is it?"

The Investigator was disconcerted by the affability in his voice and the casual tone. He smiled as he looked at the Investigator, all the while continuing to spread his pâté whose delicious smell was passing through the minute holes in the grille of the window.

"I've got Exceptional Authorisation!" announced the Investigator, holding the beermat up against the glass. The Guard glanced mechanically at the piece of card, then looked back to the Investigator.

"I'm not really sure what your Authorisation authorises you to do, but you seem extremely proud to have it, so I'm happy for you."

He downed a large draught of wine, drew one final puff on his cigarette, stubbed it out and bit into his sandwich. The Investigator watched him so enviously that the other man noticed.

"If you ask me, I'd say you're in a bad way. This hasn't been your lucky day, if I'm not mistaken?"

The Investigator nodded. This man's spontaneous kindness overwhelmed him and made him almost forget his hunger. He felt his eyes mist over.

"Go on, get back home quickly, back to where it's nice and warm, you'll only catch something dragging yourself about in weather like this. You've been exploited enough as it is, don't you think?"

The Guard gobbled down another mouthful of his sandwich. The Investigator wasn't really sure what or who this man was talking about, but he was taking some pleasure in making this brotherly moment last.

"So you're from which Department?" the Guard went on. "Cleaning? Modern slavery! Just one more! I hope at least you don't put too much effort into it? You and me, along with thousands of others, we don't mean anything to them. We're nothing. We're no more than numbers on a staff list. You could let it depress you, but I spit on it all. Look at me: the regulations state that it's forbidden to smoke, drink and eat while on duty – well, I'm doing them all at the same time. Those regulations – I really don't give a damn about them. They make us do the dirty work that nobody else wants to do? Let's do it dirtily! I'm a free man. I'll give you an example, as I can tell you are a nice guy straight away: I'm the Guard, so I'm supposed to protect The Firm from any non-authorised entry, right?"

The Investigator nodded. He was no longer in control of the movements of his body, which was being shaken by the cold. A few centimetres of snow had settled on his skull, making him a funny kind of hat. The Guard kept talking, while devouring his sandwich.

"I can assure you, hundreds of individuals could come here to steal everything there is to steal, I'd let them stroll right out without lifting my little finger, without even pressing the smallest of these emergency buttons you see here before me. I even think that I'd open the gates even wider for them, and that I'd applaud as I watched them fill their lorries with everything they've been able to steal."

The Guard drank a long draught straight from the bottle.

"I don't want to upset you, but take a look at yourself: you see the state they've got you into? And all this to bring in even more profit? If I had one piece of advice for you, in the position you're in you could sow a fine bit of chaos: rather than sweeping the floors in their offices, you could sabotage all their computers, oh, not with a sledgehammer, of course discreetly, a bit of water tipped over a keyboard, a cup of coffee in the hard disk's ventilation grille, a tube of glue in a printer, the contents of your vacuum cleaner in the air conditioning system, even a nice little short circuit here and there, the classics always work well, that's why they're classics. And that'll do the trick! The Firm is a colossus with feet of clay. Our world is a colossus with feet of clay. The problem is that few of the people like you, by which I mean the little people, the exploited ones, the hungry, the weak, the present-day serfs, have noticed. It's no longer the time for going out into the streets to cut the heads off kings. There haven't been kings for a long time. Monarchs today no longer have heads or faces. They are complex financial mechanisms, algorithms, projections, speculations about risks and losses, fifth-degree equations. Their thrones are intangible, they are screens, they are fibre-optic cables, printed circuit boards, and their blue blood is the encrypted information that circulates faster than the speed of light. Their castles have become data banks. If you break one of The Firm's computers, one among thousands, you're cutting the finger off a monarch. You understand?"

The Guard swallowed a gulp of wine and gargled with it. The Investigator had listened to him with his mouth hanging wide open. He looked like a complete idiot. The snow gave his feeble shoulders a more marked, rectangular shape. Because of it he was assuming a kind of night-time rank, the non-commissioned officer of a routed army who no longer had the slightest idea of the stakes of the conflict into which he had been thrown.

"Don't you think you ought to be careful what you say?" he ventured.

"Why careful? Because of who? I have no master. I disregard authority. People like me still exist. Why do you think I do this job everyone else refuses to do? Because I don't want to play the game. Look at me, I'm behind this glass. The whole thing is a symbol! And you're not a policeman, are you? Hm?"

"Of course not," the Investigator said.

"And you're also not that man who introduces himself as the Investigator? My colleague warned me. The man tried to force his way in last night, about ten p.m. On the pretext of an investigation into the suicides. An investigation into the suicides, at ten o'clock at night, how stupid do they think we are? I'm convinced the man is actually an Efficiency Consultant, yet another one. We get one of them every month. Each time there's a whole cartload of lay-offs. You understand, these people have no morals. They'd even come and do their thing at night if we let them, and all to carry out that revolting job of theirs! Of course you aren't the Investigator. With that miserable face of yours, your three scrawny bits of hair and your rags, you're like me, you aren't him."

"Of course . . ." replied the Investigator, who was trembling, and not only from the cold, while in the one intact pocket of his raincoat he gripped the old sausage the Watchman had given him.

"I swear to you, if that man comes back tonight," the Guard went on, "I wouldn't be as obliging as my colleague, I'd roast him!"

"You'd, er . . . roast him?"

"And without the slightest qualm! You see this lever?" the Guard said, pointing to a sort of thick rubber-covered handle on the wall. "If I lower it, twenty thousand volts shoot through all the protective metal barriers you see around you, and even if he doesn't touch them, even if he's standing right where you are now, for example, the current is so strong that in two or three seconds the repulsive creature would be transformed into a common little heap of ashes!"

"A heap of ashes . . ." the Investigator moaned.

"*Dust, to dust you shall return!*" the Guard concluded, whose chin was now adorned with a tiny bit of pâté that had fallen out of his sandwich.

# 24

THE INVESTIGATOR DID NOT USUALLY DREAM MUCH. HIS NIGHTS were peaceful, and in the morning he only remembered his dreams very rarely, apart from the recurring one with the photocopier. He was in the office. He needed to duplicate an investigation file. He went over to the place where the photocopier was, started to copy the documents in the file, but it suddenly paused because there was no ink left in the toner cartridge. As he didn't know how to change it, his function being to carry out investigations, not to take care of the maintenance of a photocopier, he waited at the machine, helpless. Very fortunately, this distressing dream had never become a reality. But this, everything he'd experienced since setting foot in this town, clearly this really was a nightmare. It couldn't not be. What else? Nothing. Yes, a nightmare. A long nightmare, admittedly of a realism that was diabolically complex, well-polished and tortuous, but a nightmare just the same!

The problem was, the Investigator couldn't see any way out. He didn't have the damnedest idea of how to escape from this quite clearly fake universe, a dream universe which wasn't in any way life. Life can't throw you like this, it can't make you meet people as troubling as those who, since the previous night, had enjoyed messing him about, starving him, disturbing him, knocking him around, making him wait, crushing him, frightening him. And yet? And yet . . . ? he asked himself. Life, which until this moment he had seen as a monotonous and pleasantly boring series of repetitions without any surprises, perhaps under certain lighting or in certain conditions could harbour unsuspected, distressing, even tragic accidents.

The street was empty, as it had been the previous evening. The cars, the crowd of pedestrians, everything had disappeared, which didn't surprise him at all, and it was just this that he found astonishing – that he was no longer surprised. He told himself that he too was beginning to espouse this illogical logic of his nightmare. This did not appease his hunger, did not bring down his fever, did not patch up his raincoat, did not relieve his immense tiredness, but all the same he did feel a little better, since if his thoughts were shaping themselves to the events he was encountering and would doubtless continue to encounter, they would, he felt, be able to bear them more easily, just as a man venturing up into high altitudes eventually gets used to the lack of oxygen.

Despite his extreme tiredness and his weakened state, it took him just a few seconds to get across the street, with an ease that made him chuckle when he remembered the struggle he'd had that same morning to get to the entrance to The Firm. He made for the Hotel, whose sign tried to light up for a few seconds, crackled to life wretchedly before going out again, then making another attempt that was doomed to failure. The road itself was completely covered with snow. There were no marks but his own footsteps. There was the proof of what he had just sensed. It was a dream snow, a dream street. It wasn't possible that not a single vehicle, not a single pedestrian had stepped through it, since this Town was not a desert: he'd seen the proof of that this morning when all those cars in their hundreds, all those pedestrians, had crammed together there in their thousands. Therefore he was dreaming.

All of a sudden he was gripped by doubt as all his reasoning began to take in water. He realised that he was playing on both planes, dream and reality, choosing one or other to explain events as it suited him. His fine theory about a nightmare was sinking like a stone. And there was only one single reality, alas, and he was sunk in it up to his neck like a stick of wood in a barrel of treacle. His morale, which a few minutes earlier had begun to recover, subsided, a fragile house of cards. He had a terrible headache again.

It was with a weary hand that he pushed open the door of the Hotel. The Giantess was behind the reception desk.

"You *used to be* in room 14?" she said when she saw him.

The Investigator wasn't able to get a single word out. He settled for shaking yes his head as he wondered what the past tense of that verb might signify. From what register had he been struck off? From what list had he been removed? And why? The Giantess was still wearing the pink towelling dressing-gown that enveloped her huge body. The Investigator felt tiny beside her, and despite his cold, and even though he was standing several metres from her, he could still sense her characteristic smell of sugary sweat.

"We've had to change your room, the Management asks you to excuse them. From now on, you're 93. First floor. Your suitcase is already waiting for you there."

The Giantess placed the tiny key down on the counter. He was about to take it, but she put her index finger down on it.

"One last thing," she said, placing her free hand on a document on the counter. "A signature on this bill for the damage you caused this morning."

"Damage . . . ?"

"I've received a report notifying me of the breakages in the women's toilets on the ground floor. I'm only passing it on. I'm not making any judgment on the fact that you entered the women's toilets . . ."

The Giantess spoke these last words more quietly, her voice full of innuendo. The Investigator almost launched into an explanation, but gave up. What good could it do? He grabbed the bill, the pen that the Giantess had put on the counter and was about to sign, but when he saw the sum that was written there he jumped.

"But that's impossible! All that for a torn towel? I refuse to sign such a thing!"

He slapped the pen down onto the counter. This had no effect on the Giantess who just continued to watch him, impassive. The Investigator was quite knocked off-balance. He took up the bill again and ran his eyes down it to read it more closely. It included fifteen headings: "*replacement of ruined towel, replacement of ruined towel-holder, replacement of ruined screws, re-plastering of damaged wall, repaint-*

ing of damaged wall, meals for three workmen (plasterer, painter, joiner), transport costs for three workmen, cleaning of the site, disinfecting of toilets, cost of incident report, cost of certified report, tax on general costs, tax on secondary costs, tax on taxes, tax on tax on taxes."

"This is a swindle! Your fake Policeman has already made me waste my time this morning and now you're trying to—"

"What fake Policeman?" the Giantess interrupted him.

The Investigator gathered his remaining strength, forced down the cloyingly sweet nausea that was rising to his lips, swallowed, pressed his hands to his temples to contain the pain banging at his skull with the stubbornness of a percussionist.

"I think you know better than I do, the man who lives in that broom cupboard over there . . ." the Investigator explained, pointing to the cubby-hole in which he'd given his statement.

The Giantess looked at the door to the broom cupboard, then back at the Investigator.

"I can't handle any of this, I've got to get some sleep . . . We'll see about this tomorrow . . . Give me back my papers and my credit card . . ."

"Where are they?"

The Investigator almost choked with panic.

"They're in the safe there, you confiscated them from me and you put them in there last night! You remember?"

The Giantess stood stock still, looked as though she had stopped breathing, and continued to stare at him.

"I don't remember. I don't remember anything when I'm

dragged from my sleep at 3.14 in the morning. And besides, 'confiscated' is not the correct term. No doubt you remember that regulation . . ."

"Paragraph 18, sub-section C . . ."

"Just so. We've already had plenty of unfortunate incidents with clients taking a room and not having the means to pay."

"Return what belongs to me – please."

The Investigator was begging. He had instilled that last word with all his distress. It seemed to have moved the Giantess. She hesitated, and then, slowly, slipped her right hand under her nightdress between her breasts, dug around a moment, and drew out a golden key, the key to the safe. She slid it into the lock, turned it three times to the left, opened the metal door, looked inside.

"Well? What is it you want back?" she asked, her voice mocking. The Investigator couldn't take his eyes off the safe.

It was shockingly empty.

## 25

THE INVESTIGATOR ALMOST LOST HIS FOOTING FOR GOOD. THERE was a long moment in which he felt his body and brain about to come apart, to crack like a wall subjected to the shaking of an earthquake, of a shockwave from a massively powerful bomb. He closed his eyes to dispel the image of an empty safe, that safe that contained precisely nothing and which was turning into a sort of complete metaphor for the situation in which he found himself, indeed for his whole life. Then he heard himself talking, his eyes still closed. Yes, the words were coming out of his mouth, like moans, weak, hesitant, ailing words, barely audible as though in their journey to reach the Giantess they'd meandered, deviated, bypassed, circumvented, endless motorways which with every fork in the road lost a little of their strength and a lot of their consistency.

"How is that possible . . . ? You've lost what I entrusted you with . . ."

The voice of the Giantess came to him in his darkness.

"That's what you say, I don't remember anything, I'll say it again, I was asleep when you arrived."

"But me . . . ? You do remember me?"

"Very vaguely, to tell the truth. And that's no proof. This evening I was told to wait for room 14. You were the only resident who had not yet returned. And so I concluded when I saw you arrive just now that you were 14. It wasn't your appearance that allowed me to deduce that, you don't look like anyone in particular."

The Investigator opened his eyes.

"Are you the only person with that key?"

"My daytime Colleague has another."

"Might he have put my credit card and my I.D. papers somewhere else?"

The Giantess paused.

"It's not likely."

"Not likely, but not impossible," the Investigator said, having reached the limit of his strength, but seeing a ray of hope.

"I'll say it again – it's not likely."

"Could we check tomorrow? I really need to sleep. I'm so weak. I haven't eaten anything. Anything."

The Giantess frowned as though suspecting some low trick.

"And how are you going to pay if you don't have anything to pay with?"

The Investigator's arms dropped to his sides. Could he, even if only for a moment, get out of this quagmire?

"I was sent here on a mission," he said, aware that the phrase might make him sound like one of those many cranks who haunt the centre of megalopolises, declaiming to anyone who'll listen that they've been sent by God or some extraterrestrial race. "I've got an

Investigation to carry out," he went on, trying to recover a more natural tone of voice, "an Investigation in The Firm that's located just opposite your establishment."

"So you're the Investigator?" the Giantess said in astonishment.

"Precisely."

The Giantess hesitated, came around her counter, approached him, took him gently by the shoulder, turned him about to examine him in detail, and pushed him over towards the large mirror occupying one wall of the entrance hall.

"Take a look at yourself."

In the glass, the Investigator saw a hunched old man, his face eaten up by a two-day beard, his hot, red eyes rolling incessantly from left to right, and right to left. His swollen forehead had turned an orangey-yellow colour, and the area immediately surrounding the wound caused by the falling telephone had turned purplish. The clothes he was wearing were ragged, crumpled, dirty, torn, most noticeably his coat, which must once have been just an ordinary off-the-peg raincoat. There was also a large tear in his trousers, at his right thigh, which appeared, white and naked, cut across with a long, zigzagging scratch spotted with dried blood. His shoes looked like pieces of brownish fluff. The sole of one of them had come detached in front and the other no longer had its shoelace.

"Who is it you're trying to convince that you look like the Investigator?"

"But I don't need to look like the Investigator, I am the Investigator!" he said, addressing both the Giantess and himself. "I am the Investigator," he said again, softly, as though really trying to convince himself, as fat tears ran down his cheeks, full, round tears, that rushed down his face, sliding onto the wrinkled skin of his neck. A child's tears. He stayed in front of the mirror a moment, unable to move, incapable of any reaction. The Giantess was back at her counter.

"Sign the bill for me, and you'll get your room. I could throw you out onto the street since you've just let me know that you aren't in a position to settle up with the Hotel, and that you don't even have a piece of I.D., but I'm not a bad woman, and I'm sure we can come to some arrangement."

He turned slowly towards the Giantess, took the pen that she was holding out to him, signed the bill without even looking at it.

"You've forgotten your key!"

He had already moved off towards the stairs. He came back, took the room key – in doing so he had to touch the Giantess's fat, clammy fingers – and went slowly up the stairs, clinging to the banister as he went.

Tomorrow he'd call. Yes, he'd make a call to his Head of Department. Too bad if he thought him stupid or incompetent, but this just couldn't go on. In any case, he wasn't going to sacrifice his health, physical or mental, still less give up his very life. He'd explain everything. The Head of Department would understand, would sort things out with the Hotel, he would stand surety and everything would be back in order. Tomorrow he'd no longer have this thorn in his foot and in his brain, and the first thing he'd do, naturally, would be to change hotel. He wouldn't spend another night in this one. He'd drive it from his life.

The Investigator had reached the door to room 93. It really was located on the first floor, just as the Giantess had told him it was. He turned the key, pushed the door, which only opened about twenty centimetres despite his repeated efforts. With some struggle he slid through that narrow gap, switched on the light, and discovered the room: a single bed, a bedside table, a wardrobe, a chair, a closed window beyond which he could see closed shutters. A door, which no doubt led to the bathroom. The same furnishings as in room 14, the same greenish walls, blistered with damp, the same round neon lamp, tired and flickering, the same photograph of the old man, so like the one on the key-ring. The only difference was the size of the room: the bed occupied almost all the space in this one, which at best covered an area of five square metres, wedging shut the door to the wardrobe as well as the one to the bathroom, which consequently it became entirely impossible to get into. As for the chair and the bedside table, since there was not enough space on the floor, they had been placed lengthwise, flat on the bed, next to his suitcase.

The Investigator shut the door behind him.

Just hang on in there, he thought, clenching his fists. Hang on . . . hang on for just one night more.

He climbed onto the bed, pushed the bedside table and the chair as far down towards the bottom of the mattress as he could. He then

gripped his suitcase, struggled to lift it because it was so heavy –
though wasn't it rather that he was so exhausted? – managed to hold
it up at arm's length, tried three times, unsuccessfully, to slide it
onto the top of the wardrobe, but gave up when he realised that the
space between the top of the piece of furniture and the ceiling was
not big enough to slip it in.

He let it drop heavily down again, but when it hit the bed it
caused to jump up – like a horned imp on a spring, from a box of
tricks and practical jokes – a little cylindrical object that till that
moment must have been hidden in a fold of the bedcover. A little
yellow and blue tube. The same one which the Policeman had
handed him that same morning and which contained the pain
medicine. The Investigator picked it up, gripped it tight, trembling,
felt a lump form in his throat. This man wasn't altogether bad,
then, as he had thought about him, as he had cared about the state
of his health, as he himself had taken the trouble to leave this
medicine on his bed. Because it couldn't have been anyone but him
who'd thought to do this. Only him.

The Investigator smiled weakly then lay down on the bed, yet
again without going to the trouble of undressing. He stretched out
along one side, curled his knees up to his chest, tucked his head into
his shoulders and closed his eyes.

He sank immediately into a deep sleep, his hands still holding
the tube of medicine and the dry sausage: an old, mummified,
inedible sausage, a tube containing tablets that he would not even
be able to absorb since he had no water and could not get access

to the bathroom, two things, in short, that were decidedly unusable, but which nonetheless bore witness to a touching human possibility in a world that seemed to him to be less and less anchored.

# 26

SOMEONE WAS RINGING. A TIMOROUS, TREMBLING, EXHAUSTED ringing. The telephone. Like the previous morning. There was a bit of daylight coming in through the closed shutters. The telephone. The Investigator opened his eyes. How small this room was, and how narrow! He felt as though he had slept in a box. The ringing continued, but he couldn't see a telephone. Damn the thing, where could it be? Nothing on the walls. Nothing on the wardrobe. Nothing on the wardrobe door, nor the bathroom door. The ringing, though extremely weak, didn't give up. Under the bed? Could someone have been so unhinged as to put a telephone under the bed? No, nothing under the bed. And that ringing, which simply did not stop. He put his ear to the door to the wardrobe that he still hadn't managed to open. No, the ringing wasn't coming from there. The ceiling? There was nothing else left but the ceiling! A telephone attached to the ceiling. The ringing persisted, timid but regular. The Investigator was on all fours on the bed. He didn't want to look up at the ceiling. He wasn't prepared to accept that someone might have planted a telephone on the ceiling. The ringing did not stop. He resigned himself to turning his head upwards slowly: the telephone was attached a little to the left of the circular neon bulb.

He leapt to his feet, stretched out his arms, tried to take hold of the receiver that was set in its base, missed it, got it on the third attempt, as the telephone yo-yoed down at the end of the flexible cable.

"Hello . . . ?"

"Hello . . . ?" replied a muffled voice, terribly far away.

"Can you hear me?" the Investigator asked.

"Can you hear me?" the voice repeated.

"Who are you?"

"Who are you?" the distant voice said.

"I am the Investigator."

"I can't take it anymore!" the distant voice replied. "I can't get it open."

"Can't get what open?"

"It's dreadful, it's absolutely impossible to open!"

"TO OPEN WHAT?!" the Investigator shouted.

"Impossible . . . I've tried everything. And this heat! Help me . . ." stuttered the voice, dying away.

"Are you still there?"

"Can't get out anymore . . . impossible."

"But get out of where? Who are you?"

"Like a rat . . ." the voice said, then fell silent.

The Investigator looked at the receiver. The telephone was still silent, but it hadn't yet been hung up. The Investigator could hear a breath, yet a breath that had nothing human about it, like the sound of the wind slipping over a desolate, flat landscape. Who had called him? Was it the same man from the day before? How could he know? And what could he do? Nothing, surely. Someone must be spying on him. All this was just a joke.

After a few seconds, he got up onto his tiptoes and replaced the receiver in the base screwed to the ceiling, and it was then, and only then, that he realised he was completely naked.

An idiotic reflex made him put both his hands flat over his crotch. But who could have observed it? The room only had one window and the closed shutters protected him from any potential peeping Toms. Besides, even though he didn't want to check, he was convinced that behind the shutters was the same wall of cemented-in breeze blocks as in room 14.

Why was he naked? He wasn't in the habit of sleeping like this. The Investigator felt so ashamed that he immediately hid under the covers, body and head. Still, he couldn't go on like this indefinitely. He wrapped himself round with the sheet, stood up on the bed, and went in search of his clothes. He had no trouble tracking down the old sausage and the tube of pills, but there was no trace of his vest, his boxers, his shoes, his shirt, his raincoat, his trousers or his jacket. Disappeared, dissolved, vanished into thin air. And yet they had to be there somewhere.

The Investigator tried to remember where he could have hidden them, but as he had no recollection of having undressed, it was all the more difficult to know what he might have done with those clothes. A violent sneeze put an end to his internal debate. Then another. Then a third. His half-blocked, oozing nose forced him to breathe through his mouth, at a faster rate than usual, which made him look like a goldfish trapped in its bowl. A boiling hot shower, or even a freezing cold one, wouldn't do him any harm. It would give him a boost, it would stimulate his mind and invigorate his body. He still needed to be able to get into the bathroom!

The Investigator stopped and thought, wrapped in his bed sheet, which gave him the look of a Roman senator, small and with a sagging belly. He came up with a plan, which he lost no time in putting into action. It involved lifting the bed up as high as possible, as far as his scant muscles allowed him, wedging the bedside table under it, then, if he still had the strength, lifting it higher still to place the chair between the bedsprings and the bedside table. The bed would then be almost vertical, thereby freeing the bathroom door.

He managed to get it open.

# 27

HE WAS ASTONISHED: THE BATHROOM WAS OF THE MOST REFINED luxury. He had not imagined that a space like it, so grand, with a floor of light marble, walls decorated with celadon mosaics topped with an ornamental frieze of cabochons gilded with fine gold, could exist within Hotel Hope, and doubtless this was the last remaining vestige of the time when the place had been a classier establishment. But the fact that this bathroom should also be the one for the room he had been given, and one that was, he could attest, the most wretched, dirty, narrow bedroom in the Hotel, well, that surpassed all understanding!

A pearly light caressed the massive gold taps of the two washbasins, the bidet, the large bathtub set into a block of porphyry, the shower, which was completely inlaid with bluish molten glass. Music that mingled the sounds of exotic birds, the shaking of a tambourine, light brass instruments imitating the noise of little coins tinkling onto a stone floor, flutes that were simultaneously high-pitched and gentle, came from multiple loudspeakers that he wasn't able to locate and which seemed to be contained within the walls. In the middle of the room, a little pool received a jet of water whose steam-encircled gurgling made the Investigator's thoughts drift to distant ports, naked black slave-girls, palm fronds being waved to cool his brow, large boats anchored in the harbour whose decks were laden with sacks of spices, pearls, amber and minerals. He'd had to read a bit of poetry when he was young, a requirement of school, but he had never understood any of it. And most of all what he hadn't understood had been the fact that men had wasted their time writing it. Because it didn't serve any purpose. None at all, while the precise, cool investigation reports that could be drafted to record acknowledged facts, to verify a truth, dissect it, draw out its conclusions, seemed a far more intelligent way – and all in all the only worthwhile way – of using language and serving humanity. Was he really so ill and disturbed that at the sight of an opulent-looking bathroom he should dream of languid negro girls, palm wine, oriental pastries and belly dancing?

A glass shelf held little bottles of multicoloured salts and liquid soaps. The Investigator opened some of them, sniffed them, but he had such a cold that it was impossible for him to smell anything at all. He contented himself with reading the labels, and decided on *Mauve Lilac*.

Dropping the sheet on the floor, naked again, but without feeling the least embarrassment about it, the Investigator tipped the whole bottle of soap into his hands, and with it covered what hair he had left, his face and body, then turned on the two taps of the shower, which immediately released a generous gush of water surrounded by a steam that was turned azure by the opalescence of the molten glass of the cubicle walls.

He put his right foot in the shower and but rapidly drew it back, crying out in pain: the water was boiling! Not hot, boiling! He turned down the flow of the hot tap a little, increased that of the cold tap, waited a moment, ventured to stick his foot back under the jet. It was even worse! He felt as though someone was pouring molten lead onto his skin. He gave up on the shower in favour of the bathtub, turned on the mixer tap, waited: steam immediately filled the block of porphyry, he no longer dared to put his foot into it. He settled for bringing his hand close to the water and confirming that here, too, it was flowing at an appallingly high temperature. There was nothing left but the washbasin and the bidet, and he hurried over to them, turning the taps towards cold. He needn't have bothered: the water that came out could have cooked an egg in thirty seconds. It was then that he looked at the piping and realised to his absolute astonishment that there wasn't a single cold water pipe feeding the various water supply points in the room.

Even the spout in the little central pool, whose steam he had taken for the product of some refined mist-producing device, gave out boiling water, as evidenced by the three Japanese carp that floated belly-up on the surface, their flesh white, cooked, and already coming apart.

All the bathroom's beauty was utterly useless. It was a Paradise heated by the flames of Hell. It was impossible to wash in it, and likewise impossible to dry himself in it as there wasn't a single towel or bathrobe. His body completely coated in *Mauve Lilac*, sticky and bloated, the Investigator felt the tiny speck of optimism that had begun to be reborn in him subside again. He bent down to gather up his bed sheet, and it was at just that moment that a door opened behind him and a fat septuagenarian man, his face bearing a substantial moustache, walked in, strolled right by him, installed himself on the toilet, unfolded a newspaper and began to read.

The Investigator didn't dare move. Where had he come from, this old man, stark naked like him, who had practically brushed past him without even noticing him, and who in every feature resembled the old man from The Firm key-ring and the immense photographic portrait from the Manager's office, and doubtless also all the reproductions hanging in the bedrooms? Was he really the same person? Hard to tell, given how different the impressions that are made by people when they are naked or clothed. And the shamelessness! It was just inconceivable! To walk in like that and settle himself on the toilet!

The Investigator was a hair's breadth away from calling out, when he said to himself that it was perhaps he who was where he shouldn't have been. What if this bathroom wasn't his? After all, hadn't he needed to make great efforts and use a certain amount of ingenuity to unblock a door that had no doubt been blocked up deliberately? Yes, of course, it was obvious . . . He was somewhere he oughtn't to be. Get out, get out as quickly as possible before the old man noticed his presence and made a scene.

The old man was immersed in his paper. There was a happy smile on his wrinkled face. The Investigator straightened up very slowly. Then, just as slowly, he slid his feet, centimetre by centimetre, along the floor towards the door to his bedroom, but he could not open it. He didn't dare insist for fear of alerting the old man who was continuing to read without paying him any attention. His salvation would be in the other exit, the very one through which the old man had come in. It was at the opposite end from the place he'd just reached at the cost of a painful creeping along on his toes, and particularly those of his right foot, which having been scalded had turned scarlet. But he had no choice. He made his way back, coated in *Mauve Lilac*, and thanks to some laboured sliding across the marble floor, reached the other door, opened it silently, and disappeared.

## 28

THE ROOM THAT HE WAS CROSSING, PRACTICALLY AT A RUN, WAS VERY different from his own. Like the bathroom he had just left, it seemed to be of the greatest refinement, vast, luxurious and comfortable. He just had time to notice an open cabin-trunk containing four or five suits, all of them apparently in the same warm, soft material, a green and beige tweed, and a large cigar which was burning itself out in an ashtray, weaving its curls of slate-grey smoke in the room's air-conditioned atmosphere.

Wrapped in his bed sheet, the Investigator found himself in the corridor. Or rather, as he quickly ascertained, in a corridor. A corridor he didn't recognise, but which most fortunately was deserted. Where was his room? To the right? To the left? By all logic it should be to the left, but seeing as nothing in the Hotel obeyed accepted rules, it was altogether probable that it was actually on the right. He tried his luck heading that way, but as he progressed, dragging his scalded right foot, he read the numbers on the door, 765, 3, 67B, 5674, 1:6, A45718, BTH2Z, which didn't give him any clue at all as to the direction of his room. He retraced his steps, passed by the door to the old man's room – ooooo@ooooo – and found that his –

93 – was right next to it. His room, which he had gone to look for following some fantastical reasoning! He went in.

The damage was catastrophic: the wooden chair had ended up smashing under the pressure of the bed, which had tipped, pivoting round, and in passing caught the telephone attached to the ceiling, which it had ripped away, as well as the fluorescent lamp, before smashing the bedside table and burying itself in the wardrobe door. This in turn, unbalanced, had fallen to one side, blocking the door to the old man's bathroom.

Exhausted, the Investigator slid down onto the floor and curled up there. His head sank into his knees. Shaken by nervous spasms, he wanted to cry, so hopeless was his situation, but his body wouldn't let him, as though it too was now on the side of those who took pleasure in tormenting him. He would have liked not to exist any longer. Yes, to disappear. How strange human desires can be sometimes. Even as men dread death, they often also see it as a solution to all their problems, without even realising that it doesn't solve anything. Nothing at all. It isn't there to solve anything. That's not what it's for.

He felt something cool against his right thigh, opened his eyes: it was the tube of pills from the Policeman. He picked it up, looked at it a moment, but without being able to come up with a single thought about it, he opened it and put all the pills in his mouth, and began to chew. Taken without water, they tasted of aromatic herbs, pleasant and fresh. He reduced them to a slightly bitter pulp which he forced down to his stomach.

The room looked like a tiny battlefield. But then what combat had it come to represent? And if there had been combat, who, then, was the victor, and who the vanquished? The Investigator pictured the bill that the Giantess would certainly be presenting him with. A good portion of his savings would go on that, no doubt. Perhaps all of them. Curiously, this possibility didn't trouble him. He always put money aside without really knowing why, without even wanting to use it. At the end of each year he would have a meeting with the Financial Adviser, a man who explained to him, with lines on graphs and diagrams to back him up, the most comfortable places for his money to snuggle away, to doze quietly like a pet, and doubtless, surrounded by all the affection and the care it needed, to reproduce in the best possible conditions. He didn't understand much of it, but ended up agreeing with what was suggested to him. Like most of his contemporaries, he was preparing himself to die with money set aside. Suddenly he realised how ludicrous the situation was. If he had a bit of money, why keep it? For whom? At the end of the day, what was it good for! And why not use it to pay for the damage?

As if to illustrate all these peculiar thoughts scratching away at his brain which was unaccustomed to such effort, the Investigator got up suddenly, grabbed the demolished chair back, and used it to destroy the place, reducing the glass of the neon bulb to powder, smashing the plastic shell of the telephone apart, ripping open the wardrobe, the mattress, the eiderdown, finally grabbing what was left of the bedside table and throwing it against the window, sending the glass tumbling into a thousand pieces onto the ravaged bed. He systematically destroyed whatever was still intact in the room, then stopped, slightly breathless, and perfectly happy.

A violent energy, emerging from some unexpected, deep place, electrified him. For the first time in his existence, he had done something gratuitous and felt no remorse for it. Quite the contrary, as he thought about the expression on the Policeman's face when shown the battlefield, he laughed a lot. He had decided to retake control of the situation, whatever it was. He had an Investigation to carry out. He would carry it out. And no half-disturbed individuals, no impossible hotel, no shameless old man, no hostile town and no firm – even The Firm itself – was going to get the better of him. Wrecking his bedroom was reasserting his freedom. History, he thought to himself, only crushes those who really want to be crushed.

He cleaned his skin as best he could with the bed sheet, removing the milky coating, which was now solidified into a brittle, whitish crust, left behind by the *Mauve Lilac*. He opened his suitcase to take out some clean clothes. The fact that it contained a drill, a set of drill-bits for wood, another for metal, another for concrete, as well as five pairs of women's knickers, two bras, a Bible in Dutch, a pair of apple-green tracksuit bottoms, rubber boots, a canary-yellow wool dress, and three handkerchiefs which he recognised as belonging to him, didn't make the slightest dent in his newly restored vitality. The bellboy who had cleared his previous room, along with others, too, no doubt, had simply mixed up the belongings of different guests before redistributing them in their luggage at random.

Without any embarrassment, the Investigator pulled on one of the pairs of knickers – synthetic, pink, see-through, trimmed with fine black lace – the tracksuit bottoms, the yellow dress which he tore down to half its length and which was transformed magically into a pleasantly warm jumper, and the pair of boots. After a slight hesitation, he finally left the drill in the suitcase, telling himself it would just get in the way. On the hook behind the door he found his raincoat, which someone had hung there. Cleaned and ironed, it was protected in a thin plastic cover. A dedicated, practised hand had mended the ripped pocket and the wide tear. A piece of paper had been affixed to the raincoat: "With the compliments of the Management."

His heart was beating nineteen to the dozen. He felt electrical discharges contracting the muscles in his body, and even those in his face as well as his eyelids, unexpectedly and deliciously. It was going to be a fine day. He was sure of it. He was no longer just a dreary, weak, drab figure, messed about by a sequence of events he didn't understand. He was no longer just the Investigator. He was becoming a hero. He had enfranchised himself, rebelled, he had taken for himself the power that others had refused to give him. The mouse was going to kill the cat. Chemistry was working wonders on him.

He left the room. As he slammed the door violently shut, the doorknob came away in his hand. He tossed it up and down a moment in his palm, carelessly, as though it were a fruit he was about to crunch into, then chucked it over his shoulder, whistling, then went down the uneven stairs, two at a time, to present himself at the breakfast hall.

# 29

"YOU'RE IN 93?" ASKED A WAITER IN A WHITE JACKET WITH BLACK trousers.

"Absolutely!" the Investigator heard himself answer, his voice revived. The Waiter gestured for him to follow him.

Once again the breakfast room was packed. But the Investigator noticed that this time it was not the same people filling it as the day before: there were a lot of families, with children of all ages, infants, and also very old people, in worn-out clothing, sometimes quite unusual outfits, huge robes trailing on the ground for some of the men, thick jackets lined in threadbare leather, faded sleeveless anoraks, black, conical overcoats, buttoned in front right down to the feet, for most of the women, scarves knotted around their heads, hand-knitted ski caps, fur caps, felt hats, shabby berets, decrepit bowlers.

They all had bundles clasped to them, leatherette sports bags, distended and depressing, cardboard boxes held together with string, huge plastic packages often reinforced with large strips of brown tape, ancient cardboard suitcases that looked as though they were about to burst. Most of them had the same physical features – an angular face, small build, a prominent nose, a complexion the colour of gingerbread, olive even, dark, curly hair, eyes that were ringed with mauve that heightened their state of palpable exhaustion even more.

A whole heap of bodies.

The Investigator couldn't get over it. There were a lot more than the previous day. The room looked as though it were about to burst from the number. And what struck him more than this was the great silence reigning, as though the tiredness of these women, these men, these children and old people, had sealed their lips and discouraged any desire they had to communicate.

They looked like peasants, or workmen, day labourers, manual workers out of a different century, beasts of burden, whose bodies, incessantly subjected to the laws of work and to the privations of food, had grown used to the thinness of a few bones and what little flesh covered them. Everything about them betrayed poverty, destitution, as well as the dread that this condition, suffered no doubt for decades, centuries even, had ended up depositing deep down in all their movements and their looks, like a genetic trait against which there was no point fighting. The same mark of suffering was imprinted on each one of these people. But there was nothing to make it possible to determine their origins clearly, the exact country that was theirs.

Most of them were clustered together around tables that were supposed to be for four. The skinny children who didn't have places for themselves were held on the laps of adults who were barely bigger than they were. They were nibbling on rusks. And beside those rusks, which the Investigator recognised as the same as those vile things he had been forced to eat the previous day, there were also little cups of black coffee, barely filled with that muddy beverage the very memory of which made him nauseous. In this way all the people, regardless of age or sex, who were of an inhuman thinness, were forced to suffer the same fate: a dry diet.

"Tourists?" the Investigator asked.

"You're kidding! Them, Tourists? Have you seen them? Have you given them a sniff?" the Waiter said.

"Please, not so loud, they'll hear you!" the Investigator muttered.

"None of them can understand us, they're not from here. I don't know what language they speak, but one thing's for sure it isn't ours. They're The Displaced."

"The Displaced?"

"Yes, The Displaced." And as the Investigator had shown his surprise, the Waiter thought it worth adding:

"But what planet have you been living on? For months we've been turning them away, whole batches of them, but they keep coming back, and more numerous than ever: have you noticed how many children these women make? If we could do without, we would, gladly, but the Hotel is requisitioned by Repatriation Services almost every other day. Look at them: do you think they're unfortunate? They're different, that's all. I hate different. And I love disinfectants. You, for example, your scent is particularly fine, and so I find you likeable. Here, you're over there: I managed to keep you a table. The Management has asked me to tell you they regret having to inflict this spectacle and this smell on you. I'll bring you your breakfast right away."

The Investigator sat down at the table the Waiter had indicated: four places surrounded by empty chairs. All around him, the other tables were occupied with families, men, women squeezed against one another, but the place awaiting the Investigator resembled a protected or forbidden little island. The same space that he enjoyed to himself, a few metres away was allocated to about twenty people on average, who were all evidently placed here in the greatest discomfort. He took his seat without looking about him too much, lowered his head and waited.

He did try to remember, but he'd never heard of this phenomenon before. "The Displaced"? Indeed, he wasn't unaware of the reality of certain population movements, nor the attraction that his continent exercised on a lot of people. But The Displaced?

"93?"

The Investigator didn't have the leisure to ruminate any further. Two Waiters were standing in front of him. Both had uttered the number of his room simultaneously. The Investigator nodded. With one movement the Waiters put two large trays down on the table, wished him a "*bon appétit*" and disappeared into the Crowd which opened with difficulty before them, but closed back up again very quickly like two hands wanting to keep their warmth held tightly in their palms.

# 30

FOUR THICK RASHERS OF BACON, THREE WHITE SAUSAGES, TWO *andouillette* sausages with herbs, a streaky-bacon omelette, four soft-boiled eggs, six herring fillets pickled in onion vinegar, sweet and sour gherkins, smoked salmon sprinkled with dill, reindeer meatballs, a jar of potted meats, an assortment of cheeses, a basket of pastries, a half-pound of butter, toasts, aniseed bread, poppy-seed bread, sesame bread, honey, quince marmalade, rose petal jam, a cheesecake, a jug of apple juice, a bowl of fresh fruit salad, bananas, peaches, strawberries, a pineapple, five kiwis, a large pot of smoked black tea, another of bergamot-scented tea. And not a single rusk! Not even a little foul black coffee! The Investigator could not believe his eyes. So many delicacies set down on his table, he who was so hungry, his belly so hollow. His head was spinning from all that food. He felt drunk. He did not know where to start, but he really had to, since he was afraid the Waiters would change their minds, or would realise they had made a mistake and come over to take the trays back.

He threw himself onto the croissants, the omelettes, the herb sausages, the poppy-seed bread. He stuffed it all into his mouth with his fingers, he was barely chewing, swallowed everything whole, choking on his food, poured himself cups of steaming tea that he drank in one gulp, dunked his fingers in the honey, pulled apart a salmon steak coated with quince marmalade, dipped a *pain au chocolat* in the jar of potted meats, soaked up the marinade from the herrings with the bacon, wiped his lips with a piece of toast, then crammed it in his mouth, chewed on two bananas at once, pecked at a reindeer meatball. He felt his belly filling like a barn being crammed with grain after harvest time. He smiled as he devoured, stuffed himself without keeping count, his head down over the bowls, plates, cups, abandoning any dignity, not worrying in the least about the sauces running down the side of his mouth, the stains on his jumper, the state of his fingers, which had been reduced to greasy claws. And to think that he had been hungry, so hungry he could have wept. A distant memory. He smiled, as he stuffed himself.

"Nothing else you need?"

The first Waiter had just appeared. At the sound of his voice, the Investigator looked up.

"Everything is very good," the Investigator said, gesturing towards the carnage he had already perpetrated on the two trays.

"Really don't hesitate," the Waiter went on. "If there's anything at all you need, that's what we're here for."

He gave a bow, turned, elbowed his way through and disappeared behind the screen of bodies congregated around the Investigator's table. It was a human wall that was now a few centimetres away from him. A densely packed masonry of eyes, hands, mouths, faces squeezed against one another, a large beseeching wall of The Displaced, watching him. He was surrounded: old people, young people, men, women, children and adolescents, all stuck to one another, one on top of another, countless tiers deep, three or four layers superimposed in a living mass grave and they were watching him and their wide-eyed stare spoke of their appal-ling hunger, their wish to eat, their desire to kill, too, perhaps, for a bit of bread, a piece of sausage, a slice of hard-boiled egg.

The closest one to him was a child. He might have been four years old, or five, maybe even ten, but he was so thin that he no longer had an age. The Child looked at the Investigator. He was a little human being who was barely alive – nearly dead, as a matter of fact – whose disproportionately swollen belly was bumping against the table on which the food was accumulated. He did not ask for anything. He just settled for watching the Investigator with his empty eyes. He watched him from the depths of his exile. He was no longer just one of The Displaced. He was also the Witness.

The Investigator dropped the bit of sausage he still had in his fingers. This could not go on. He struggled to swallow what he had in his mouth. His belly hurt. He was suffocating. All these people were so close. Too close to him. He could not get enough air. And the Child stared at him, as the others stared at him, but the Child especially, with something in his pupils that pressed down on the Investigator's soul like an engraver's point on a copper plate, and this point calmly wrote on it, interrogating, questioning.

There was no longer any sound to be heard. The Investigator undid the large napkin he had tied around his neck, dropped it onto the table, which was still completely cluttered with food, then got up slowly.

And yet it had all started so well.

"Leaving us already?" one of the Waiters enquired as he passed through the doorway, after the crowd of The Displaced had gradually parted in his path, as one would do before gods or lepers. The Investigator did not even reply. He was holding his belly with both hands and gritting his teeth. He wanted to vomit, but felt that he would never be able to get everything out, give everything up. Because you can never give everything up, he thought. Never. Just as you probably cannot live happily without stealing the happiness of someone living somewhere else. He was shivering. He felt as heavy as a manhole cover, his scalded foot was tapping on the inside of his boot, and now, to cap it all, he was turning philosopher. A poor, banal philosopher, quite insignificant, who wore woman's knickers and apple-green tracksuit bottoms, spouted thoughts that were worthless and worn-out like old saucepans that have grown tired of cooking the same soup day after day.

## 31

SOMEONE WAS DRUMMING ON THE DOOR OF THE TOILET CUBICLE in which he had locked himself.

He had just had time to flee the breakfast room, cross the reception hall, spot a door he hadn't noticed before, and on which he'd read the inscription "Men's Toilets", to rush in, and vomit lengthily what he had earlier managed to swallow. He was, what was more, still on all fours, his head half-inside the toilet bowl. Someone was drumming harder and harder.

"Coming . . ." he managed to say. His voice echoed as though in a cave. He got up reluctantly, wiped his mouth with toilet paper then unbolted the door.

"Ah, well then!" the Policeman was standing opposite him. Dressed in a mauve overall with white spots, in one hand he held a long-handled brush, in the other a blue bucket filled with sponges and cleaning products.

"Sorry, I wasn't very well . . ." the Investigator groaned.

The Policeman eyed his outfit, but made no comment.

"I haven't done any damage, you needn't worry, and I haven't got anything dirty either. See for yourself."

The Policeman's expression hardened abruptly.

"I haven't asked you a thing. I was concerned about you. I saw you dash into the toilets while I was busy finishing off a report, with the door to my office ajar, as the air gets very stuffy in there, and you behave as though I were just doing my job! What do you take me for? You think you're the only person who cares about other people's misfortune? You think the distressing psychic and sanitary condition of The Displaced doesn't bother me as much as it does you? While I am indeed the Policeman, I'm no less of a man for it. And even if I don't throw up my breakfast like you've done, their kind does affect me, and I do everything I can to make their Displacement as quick as I can so that in as little time as possible they can find their way to the place that is theirs and which they'll never have to leave. Now, shift yourself, I've got things to do."

The Investigator turned over in his head what the Policeman had just said, but the man – his hands protected by a pair of pink rubber gloves – after having sprayed the toilet bowl with a yellow liquid that gave off fumes of bleach and pine resin, was scrubbing at the ceramic with a sponge and all the energy he could muster.

"You aren't a Policeman. This place isn't a high-end luxury hotel. This is not reality. I'm in a novel, or in a dream, and what's more certainly not in one of my own dreams but in someone else's, someone complicated, perverted, who's enjoying himself at my expense."

The Policeman got up, fixed his stare on the Investigator,

seemed to stop and think and then finally dropped the sponge in the bucket – which made a strange sound, like a quick sigh. He slowly pulled off his gloves, all the while contemplating the Investigator.

"Follow me."

The words were said without aggression, almost sweetly. The Investigator, still surprised at the sentiments that had come out of his mouth and the tone in which he had expressed them, was a breath away from apologising. He preferred to stay silent and follow him.

"I imagine this morning you're getting ready to return to The Firm to carry out your Investigation there?"

The Policeman had stopped on the front steps of the Hotel. It was an identical morning to the previous one. Mild, caressed by a golden light, filled with intense human activity. The two pavements unfurled their concentrated, compact Crowd, and the road disappeared under the stream of cars that rolled by at walking speed, tightly packed against one another, without any of the drivers seeming to complain about the slowness of their progress.

"Clement morning, fierce evening."

"Excuse me?"

"I was referring to the climate," the Policeman explained. "Like you, I was a bit surprised at first. You just can't understand it. A certain air of spring – or even summer – in the early hours of the day, and unfailingly towards the end of the afternoon, snow, then the freeze that tears at your face in the evening, and finally that early night time that drops like a guillotine. It could be a metaphor for life, but I'm not the Poet, I'm only the Policeman.

"You set too much store by appearances. I wonder how you could be capable of carrying out an Investigation, whatever it is, with so little clear-sightedness. You see me in a cleaning woman's overall, a brush in my hand, you jump to conclusions. And because my office resembles a broom cupboard, you tell yourself I'm a simple cleaner who has lost his reason. No, don't protest! That's just what you thought, they've told me. What a lack of imagination on your part! I could be offended. I could have arrested you then and there, after yesterday I'm not short of motives. I could have used my arbitrary, limitless power torturing you some way or other, but I believe in the virtues of pedagogy. Come."

The Policeman crossed the pavement with disarming ease. The Crowd parted instantly into two separate waves. The men and women veered aside at his approach, rushed to let him by. No-one brushed past him. Having thus effortlessly reached the edge of the pavement, he turned to savour the Investigator's reaction. Open-mouthed, the Investigator stared at him as though he had witnessed a miracle. The Policeman noticed this, smiled at him and shrugged as if to say that he had not seen anything yet. He turned towards the road, simply raising his arm as his left foot stepped onto the tarmac. At once all the vehicles came to a halt. It was an astonishing sight. It was as though a sea had split violently into two, revealing its rocky bed – in this case it happened to be a common tarmac surface, pitted with ruts here and there – driving its waves away on both sides. The Policeman crossed the road in a few seconds and set foot on the opposite pavement where – here, too – the Crowd took the greatest care to avoid him.

"Do you need any further proof that I'm really the Policeman?" he called out to the dumbfounded Investigator. The latter's brain was turning into a dwarf mammal caught in a wheel it was spinning at full speed, producing nothing but gratuitous, unnecessary, meaningless movement and a dramatic amount of overheating.

"Join me!" the Policeman shouted.

Like a robot, the Investigator obeyed, crossed the pavement, then the road, under the silent protection of the Policeman who was watching over the manoeuvre and continuing to hold cars and pedestrians at a standstill under his authority. When he had reached him, and as, with a simple click of his fingers, the Policeman had made the traffic start up again, the Investigator stood beside him, head hanging down, ashamed, and, after a silence that lasted an eternity, he murmured, sheepishly:

"Please accept my apologies."

# 32

"YOU'RE NOT THE FIRST TO MAKE THAT MISTAKE. OF COURSE, IT was different before: everything was clear. But I'm not a man to lament the past," the Policeman concluded magnanimously, shaking the hand of the Investigator who was suddenly even more ashamed and looked down.

"I have something to confess to you."

"Come now, I've already told you that—"

"It's important for me," the Investigator cut in. "I've got to tell you: this morning I ransacked my room. I devastated it. I broke everything. I don't know what came over me. It was stronger than me, or rather, I wasn't myself, I'm naturally shy and sweet-tempered, but this morning I was transformed into a monster, a violent animal. Looking back on it, I think I would have been capable of killing."

His eyes were still fixed on the ground, ready to undergo a long questioning, a reconstruction, a lengthy custody, but the Policeman immediately adopted an easy-going tone:

"Come now, you do like doing yourself down! Killing! The things you say! My job has taught me killing isn't that simple. It's not something just anyone can manage. Without wanting to hurt your feelings, you haven't got it in you to be a murderer. There's a reason you were named the Investigator. You weren't judged suitable to be the Killer. Stick to your proper function. As for your room, don't trouble yourself over it! They showed it to me while you were having breakfast. It's true that you didn't pull any punches, and you were right to do what you did! It was unworthy of you. It's the fault of the person who dared to put you in that room. No-one's going to be squabbling with you over a bit of hurly-burly like that! Case closed! And anyway, I've already made my report, and the Culprit will pay the price, I can assure you of that."

"But who's the Culprit?"

"I'm taking care of that. I'll find out. And if I don't find them, I'll make them up. I'm quite formidable at what I do. I forbid you from worrying about this another second: you have a far more important mission to conduct. You are the Investigator."

The two of them had arrived at the Guardhouse. The Policeman had insisted on accompanying him there. He rang the bell himself and spoke to the Guard – the same one as the previous morning? In any case, he was physically identical – advising him to treat the Investigator well.

"He's a friend," the Policeman explained.

Friendship is a rare thing, one which the Investigator had never felt. Many human beings pass through their existence without ever experiencing this feeling, just as others bypass love, while for them it is a frequent, banal, everyday occurrence to experience indif-ference, rage, hatred, to be driven by envy, jealousy, the spirit of revenge.

Was the Policeman thinking about what he was saying, or was it just a simple formula? the Investigator wondered. He was still standing at the Guardhouse, his right hand caressing the new yellow and blue tube of pills that he had just been given by his parting friend, as the spotted overall disappeared into the Crowd, and with it the person who wore it.

The Guard was waiting, smiling, behind the glass. The Investigator turned towards him, gestured with his head in the direction the Policeman had left, and heard himself say:

"He's a friend."

As he spoke these words, the Investigator felt a pleasant wave being born in his belly, a wave which rose gradually towards his heart, his lungs, then his soul.

"I'm sorry, but I still haven't recovered my I.D. papers," he went on.

"No problem," the Guard replied, "you're a friend of the Policeman. I'll call the Guide. Would you make your way, please, towards the entrance?"

Without a doubt, the Investigator said to himself, everything is going as well as I could have hoped this morning: the sun is doing its job as the sun. The weather is fine. The behaviour of my interlocutors is strictly normal. I can even hear birds singing. The world is in its place and turning just as it should.

Less than an hour earlier, the Investigator had been gobbling down kilos of food under the eyes of starving, frightened, exiled creatures, whom someone was preparing to send back to their misfortunes, then he had brutally thrown up the whole lot, gripped by a violent feeling of guilt and shame that he was neither able to master nor to silence. He had been so weak and disorientated that he had even come to doubt the existence of the universe in which he was moving, and the solidity of the beings he was coming across, but it had only taken a road crossed without difficulty, a kind word spoken by a man, the Policeman, whom to be frank he barely knew, the smile of an employee separated from him by a glass screen, a ray of light and an air of springtime for him to forget other people's suffering, his helplessness, his fever, the pain in his forehead, his loneliness, his Investigation and even his hunger. The Investigator was experiencing forgetfulness, which prevents a lot of men from dying too quickly.

The Sentry was coming to meet him. And there was no doubt about it, it was definitely the same one as the day before. The Investigator's good mood took a knock. The memory of the arrogant indifference of this muscular creature suddenly tarnished the brightness of his start to the day.

"Had a good night? Sleep well?"

The Sentry was still two heads taller than him. He was still dressed in his perfectly pressed paramilitary jumpsuit, with the same tools for communication, attack and defence still hanging from his belt, but he looked at the Investigator with a benevolent gaze, his mouth open in a smile of an almost supernatural whiteness.

"I must have seemed a little hard on you, yesterday, but what do you expect, that's my job. Yours is to investigate, mine is to be on the look-out, and no-one will ever seriously believe you're vigilant if you don't wear a forbidding expression, along with a whole range of lucky charms – " with his large hands he gestured towards all the things hanging from his belt – "all quite useless, actually. I spend my working hours silencing my feelings, hiding them, nipping them in the bud, while yesterday, for example, there was only one thing I wanted: to hold you tight in my arms."

"To . . . hold me tight in your arms . . . ?" the Investigator babbled.

"You didn't suspect a thing, right? Not to boast, but I'm a good actor. I thought about it all night. I felt bad for not having done it. Regrets, they're a terrible thing. My life is burdened down with regrets, and I find it harder and harder to live with them. I can tell what other people think from the way they look at me. I'm a uniform, a sort of brute doing the job of a brute. They look at me like I'm an animal, just a heap of muscles, a beast without a brain. But I have a brain, and above all, I have a heart. A heart that beats, that needs love. Did you know that at night, when I take off this uniform and these pendants, when I find myself alone and naked, that I cry? Like a punished or abandoned child. When I saw you yesterday I felt you could understand me. I felt that you were like me, that we were similar to one another. And I wasn't wrong?"

The Investigator was flabbergasted.

"Tell me, was I not wrong?" the Sentry went on, begging.

The Investigator made a vague gesture that might have passed for encouragement.

"I was sure of it. Last night I swore to myself that if the opportunity ever presented itself again I wouldn't manufacture yet another regret for myself. Which is why, if you have no objection, I'd love to hold you tight in my arms, right here, right now. It's not every day that one gets to meet an investigator, who what's more is the Investigator, someone with a leading role, while me, I'm a nobody, a silhouette called in at the last minute and then quickly forgotten, a secondary being. That is my destiny. I created it for myself. I accept it."

In fact, the Investigator said to himself, this might be another kind of torture. Extreme kindness, excessive, unjustified, ridiculously hyperbolic friendliness, combined with brutality, ill-treatment, indifference, squabbles, absurdity. Yet again I'm being put to the test, he thought. I'm being made fun of. I'm being studied. I'm just a toy whose performance is being tested before it's placed on the market. No doubt about it, I'm being watched from somewhere. But who? The Head of Department? His Boss? The Boss of the Boss of the Head of Department? The Manager? The Guide who is also the Watchman? The Policeman who professes himself my friend? The Giantess with the stranglehold on the Hotel? God? Someone more important than God? All my reactions are being recorded. Doubtless I'm in the middle of a process of verification, right in the middle of a tortuous process of quality control, watched by a whole team of men in white, Scientists, Censors, Judges, Arbitrators, and I don't know who else. I'm supposed to be the Investigator, but aren't I myself at the centre of another Investigation, substantially larger than me and whose stakes are considerably more vital than in the one I am to carry out myself?

"Well?" the Sentry asked, in an ecstasy.

"Well what?"

"Can I hold you in my arms?"

It was in truth a strange scene, and moreover one that nobody witnessed. The huge Sentry with the Minotaur's brow clasping the weak Investigator, wrapping him in his huge arms, holding him close for a long moment, practically smothering him, as in a final desperate attempt to test whether a person is alive, his affinity, his belonging to the same species, the certainty of being chained to the same bench on the same galley.

It was the crackling in the Sentry's earpiece that put an end to the embrace. As if called back to attention, he suddenly stopped clinging to the Investigator and took two steps backwards, his face returning to his former expression, hard and serious. He listened. And the Investigator, who had come very close to being smothered to death, was finally able to get his breath back.

Someone was talking to the Sentry, at length. They were explaining something to him. From time to time he would reply, always the same way, repeating the word "Affirmative" or the phrase "Received loud and clear", alternating with one another like a juggler does with balls or clubs.

He towered over the Investigator, and the Investigator said to himself that this man was the only one of his interlocutors who was so big, massive, young, his hair so thick, while the others answered to the same physical type – smallish, baldish, rather middle-aged – which, what was more, was his own type, too. This observation did not help him at all. Men often think things whose immediate usefulness is not apparent to them, and which in many cases turn out not to have any at all. But sometimes thinking is like running a washing-machine on empty: while it is a useful exercise for testing that it works, the dirty linen that has been left outside the machine remains so for ever in spite of everything.

# 33

THE INVESTIGATOR WAS FOLLOWING THE GREEN LINE. HE WAS
doing what the Sentry had told him to do, and the Sentry had told
him to do what he had been told to tell him. So it was all clear.
Someone had made a decision, and that decision was in operation,
as evidenced by the scrupulous journey of the Investigator, never
deviating far from the green line, taking supreme care to put both
feet on the strip which had been perfectly executed on the ground by
a man who once upon a time had been given the mission of painting
this coloured strip, and who had done it, without seeking to know
why he had been ordered to do it nor what purpose it served.

The Investigator walked on. Where, he didn't know, but this did
not bother him. He had swallowed all the pills at once from the new
tube he'd been given by his friend the Policeman and he chewed
them with pleasure, savouring their bitterness and their subtle
aroma of medicinal plants.

He thought kindly of the Policeman, the Sentry, and also of the
Guide in relation to what the Sentry had informed him – this, too,
was something he had been told to tell him – that the man was the
victim of a Level 6 Hindrance and would not be able to come and

meet him this morning. When the Investigator asked what a Level 6 Hindrance was, the man replied he did not know a thing about it, and that it didn't fall within the framework of his function to know this, his mission being limited to ensuring that no unauthorised visitors should penetrate The Firm's outer wall. Order does not exist without the concept of society. People often think it is the opposite, but they are wrong. Man created order while no-one was asking him for anything. He thought he was being smart. It was a bad move.

Not walking very quickly, the Investigator was allowing himself to be taken over by strange theoretical analyses. He also let a group of thirty-seven people overtake him – eleven women and twenty-six men, of Asian origin, helmeted and wearing the white overall as well as the External Element badge, who were themselves following the red line at a brisk pace. He envied them. Not for following the red line, but for wearing the helmet and overall. He missed that. The overall could at least have allowed him to hide the apple-green tracksuit bottoms and the re-stitched raincoat, and the helmet would have made him look serious, professional, which he didn't think he looked anymore. But the Sentry had not been able to help him with any of this plan: he didn't have an overall or a helmet in his possession. It was the Guides who supplied the External Elements.

The Asian group was no more than a memory on the horizon. The Investigator continued to follow the green line. He was glad to have a goal. His cold had abated, even if his swollen, scarlet nose, a real clown's appendage, remained painful, just as his scalded foot was painful, rubbing against the inside of his boot, and the wound on his forehead which was starting to heal thanks to a sort of brownish crust whose pattern reminded him of a bishop's crosier or the tail of a scorpion.

The Investigator had assumed the demeanour of a *flâneur*. He wouldn't have looked out of place in the landscape of an October Sunday morning, on the banks of a canal wreathed in a luminous mist whose densest parts, compact as tow, clung to the blond branches of the old poplar trees.

But the tranquil appearance was deceptive: the truth was that the Investigator did not miss a thing that he saw in his surroundings. His vision seemed to have become sharper, and all his senses more awake. The imminent start to his Investigation was acting as a drug. His modestly built body, with its weak muscles, its supreme flabbiness, seemed reinvigorated by a new energy. He was going into action. He was going back to being himself.

He made a mental note of all the buildings they passed. With a precise command of detail and remarkable scope as regards the general layout, he was able to reconstruct in his mind a three-dimensional model of the part of The Firm he was walking across. He was not convinced that this exercise would prove hugely useful in his future as an Investigator, but at least it demonstrated his capacity to detach himself from direct, material things to be able to conceive the simplification of physical structures using varied materials, bricks – molybdenum, carbon steel, photovoltaic cladding – constructed at different times.

What was happening to him? Why all these thoughts? None of them were like him. What mouth was it, talking in this skull? He stopped. He was sweating. He remembered the Office Accountant. He recalled having heard her once talking to a Secretary about voices she would hear from time to time, voices that told her to do this or that, to wear patent leather pumps on Fridays, to eat chicken three times a week, to run across the park humming a fashionable tune, to lean out from her balcony and show her bare chest to the old man who lived opposite. The Investigator, hiding behind the coffee maker, had heard this and had been stunned.

Could it be that he was also the victim of his own private voices? He tried in vain to listen out, he could not hear anything, nothing but the buzzing of The Firm, a sort of monotone music like the sound of an electrical transformer. And yet, all these thoughts he could not get rid of, this vocabulary that was invading him in a succession of tides and waves were not his. And if someone – something? – was starting insidiously to enter and inhabit him, interfering in his brain, his body, his movements and his words, how in such a situation was he to go back to being himself as he had believed himself to be a few minutes earlier?

The Investigator forced himself to stop thinking. He also stopped looking around him. He gradually accelerated his pace and fixed his gaze on the green line as though it were the guarantee of his salvation. He began almost to run, eyes on the strip, the strip that represented the thread of his life and his destiny, the strip he saw as a safety-protection device. He sped up further, his heart went wild in his chest, his breathing got shorter, the sweat ran down his forehead, down his back, between his shoulder-blades, in his armpits, the back of his neck. He sped up more and more, ran himself breathless, ran as though his survival depended on it, his eyes attached themselves to the green line, the green line replaced all thought, the green line sucked up his grey cells, kneaded them, made them change colour, gave them shades of celadon, jade, emerald, olive, forest green.

The collision was terribly violent. The Investigator, his head down, hurtling full throttle, pepped up by the pills from his friend the Policeman, had just crashed dramatically, and with no attempt to brake, against a wall of thick breeze blocks at the foot of which the green line ended. He was now lying on the ground, unconscious. His body limp. His brain activity paused. A bump was appearing on his forehead, in the very same place as his scar, which had reopened and from which came a trickle of dark blood.

The temperature began to drop and the sky covered over. Heavy clouds, weighty as barges, seemed to have agreed to meet there: in they flowed from all sides, driven by angry winds. It was not long before they collided, crashed, they were disembowelled and the first drops of icy rain fell on the Investigator, still passed out, who didn't even feel them.

# 34

YES, ON THIS OCCASION THE INVESTIGATOR MADE NO MISTAKE: FOR a few hours, he was busy dreaming. A true dream, that is, one constructed by the mind when it is at rest, when it has nothing to do, when – lazy, unemployed – it isn't looking for something to occupy itself with, coiling up in its idleness and refusing any offers of activity suggested to it. A real dream whose nonsense, most of the time, does itself bear parabolic witness to the harmful consequences of the absence of work in any individual.

The Investigator was reviewing The Firm's Suicides. They had brought them to him in a room, and lined them up for him on the floor, side by side: twenty-two bodies and an urn, one of them having been cremated.

The Suicides still bore the marks of their final acts. Seven had a rope around their neck and their tongue sticking out. Six had their temples exploded by a revolver shot. One had its throat slit, while for three others it was the veins on their wrist, two were charred following their self-immolation, the face of one was totally cyanotic, the head still in the plastic bag in which they had suffocated themselves, and two were still trickling the water from the river in which they had drowned.

All of them were resolutely dead, there was no doubt about that, and yet each of them followed the Investigator with their eyes as he walked up and down in front of them and studied them closely and professionally. This sight which might have been fearsome did not trouble him in the least. He likewise found it quite normal that the Suicides should reply to all his questions on the processes of their suicides, their motivations, whether their successes had been preceded by one or more other attempts, why these attempts had failed. Up to this point, the Investigator had rather neglected the urn, but when he asked who had died from gas, it was the urn who replied, and the fact that an urn was starting to talk did not seem in the least preposterous.

"Me, sir."

"Please, call me Mr Investigator."

"Very well, Mr Investigator."

"You're the one with the gas, then?"

"Yes."

"One question, then: was it an accident or suicide?"

"A bit of both, Mr Investigator."

"How so? That's impossible."

The urn seemed to hesitate, then went on:

"I meant to commit suicide. I'd taken my decision. But I wanted to throw myself out of the window. But I didn't have the time. The explosion happened just before I jumped."

"At your place?"

"At my place. I'd made myself a coffee to give myself courage. I must have put out the flame, but forgotten to turn the knob shut. I hesitated a long time before taking the plunge, if I might use that expression. The gas escaped. I didn't smell a thing, my nose is always blocked up, I get all sorts of allergies, especially to hazel pollen and silver birch pollen, to dust mites, as well as cat hair, allergies that have poisoned my existence since I was a teenager. I can see myself climbing onto the window ledge, releasing the catch, and then boom, and then nothing."

"Boom?"

"Yes. Boom, Mr Investigator. A big boom. It's the last memory I carry with me from the world of the living."

The Investigator thought for a few moments, looked at the urn for some time, and realised that all the other Suicides were following the conversation attentively, no doubt waiting to hear the Investigator's conclusion.

"Well, that makes no difference to me, since you wanted to commit suicide and you are dead."

"Not wanting to waste your time, if I may, I don't altogether agree with you, Mr Investigator," the urn demurred. "I am indeed dead, but I didn't die at all the way I wanted to. And I'd like to draw your attention to the fact that I died a few seconds before I was able to commit suicide. So it isn't technically a suicide."

"But you did fall out of the window all the same?"

The Investigator, seeing the urn's awkwardness at answering him, told himself that he'd just scored a point.

"Yes . . . That's undeniable, but . . . what did I die of, really? From my fall? From a heart attack following the terror provoked by the explosion, or from the explosion itself, which would have ripped through my lungs and all my organs, bringing almost instant death, and in any case a death that preceded the moment when my skull hit the ground?"

"You tell me! What showed up on the autopsy report?"

"There wasn't one. My wife had me cremated even before the Police or The Firm had the time to order one."

The Investigator was dumbfounded. In this case, then, it was impossible to determine whether it was suicide or an accident. The statistical chart he wanted to attach to his Investigation report did not anticipate a scenario like this. Uncertainty is intolerable in the realm of statistics. The seriousness of his work was going to be discredited because of it, and he himself, as a result, severely weakened.

The urn fell silent. You could tell the urn itself felt bad at having put the Investigator in such a tricky position. The Suicides looked away. They all sensed the growing unease to which the Investigator was victim. The moment stretched forever, seemed like it would never come to an end.

An unbearable pain pulled him out of it.

"Don't move! I'll be gentle."

A woman was standing over him. A woman he'd never seen before, but whose features were familiar to him: round, ageless, with fine hair. She was wearing a white overall. To all appearances she seemed to be a nurse or a doctor.

"What happened to me?" asked the Investigator, yanked brutally out of his dream, the smallest parts of his skull concentrating the pain at near unprecedented levels.

"You bumped into the wall, it happens a lot when someone is distracted. Most people get away with just a bump, but you must have been running like a madman, I presume, to have got yourself into this state. You were gathered up completely unconscious. All the same, you were luckier than the Korean."

"What Korean?"

"Two months ago. But he must have been going even faster than you, those people throw a lot of energy into the things they do. That's what's led to their economic strength. The result was a Level 7 Hindrance."

"Meaning?"

"Death," the woman went on, distractedly, injecting something into the Investigator's arm.

"All I did was follow the line . . . " he murmured as if to himself, thinking about the faceless Korean, telling himself he'd just narrowly escaped the same fate.

"The problem," the woman went on, "is that everyone follows that line without any discrimination. When you look up you can see perfectly well that it leads straight into the wall. It's the result of a painting error, or a subtle attempt at sabotage, we'll never know: the Employee who once painted it misunderstood his orders, or wanted to misunderstand them, and rather than making it turn off towards the right in order that it lead people to my office, he made it go into the wall, and even continued it on the wall itself, for two metres of it, anyway, as high as he could reach with his paintbrush, and he ended it with an arrow pointing towards the clouds. Your case, like that of the Korean, is an extreme one, but do bear in mind that I've seen certain people who once they get close to the wall don't dare to move away from it, try to scale a five-metre wall, a wall without anything to hold on to and which ends in a roll of barbed wire, until they've torn the skin on their fingers and broken their nails, and to go where? Into the sky? You understand the conditioned behaviour that men in certain circumstances can assume, when they have to obey instructions, guidelines or directives."

All this reasoning was a little complicated for the Investigator, who, feeling his head so bruised, had clung to certain elements – the line on the wall, the death of the Korean, the Level 7 Hindrance – and not to others, which for the moment were too abstruse for him.

"What level Hindrance would you call mine?"

The woman looked at him, felt his forehead, which made him cry out in pain, took his pulse, examined the whites of his eyes.

"Our scale for evaluating Hindrances goes from Level 1, which consists of missing two minutes of work to go to the toilet, up to 7, signifying the irreversible stopping of a person's vital functions. At first glance, and naturally without this being able to be used for a claim from an insurance company or in a tribunal as part of a legal action taken against The Firm, I'd say your case is a Level 3 Hindrance, but that, I should repeat, is not a real diagnosis, some cranial fractures, for example, are undetectable in a superficial examination but this doesn't prevent them leading a few hours later to a rapid death."

The Investigator thought of the Guide, who the Sentry had told him had suffered a Level 6 Hindrance. He couldn't stop himself asking this woman to what this Level 6 corresponded.

"Cessation of brain function."

The Investigator began to tremble. A lump came to his throat. What could possibly have happened to the Guide?

"Thank you, Doctor . . ." he groaned.

"You shouldn't feel bad about the mistake, but I'm not actually a doctor, I'm a psychologist," replied the woman, smiling, and in that smile it was as though he had seen his own reflection in a mirror, a reflection with a bit of lipstick, a bit of light eye-shadow and slightly more hair.

The Psychologist stood up.

"I think you're in a state to follow me now. We're going to move into my office."

# 35

THE INVESTIGATOR ALLOWED HIMSELF TO BE TAKEN BY THE ARM and led like a sick child. They left the room, which might have resembled an infirmary. As they walked, he noticed he was no longer wearing his raincoat, nor his tracksuit trousers, but the simple gown of a hospital patient, salmon-coloured, in a light and pleasant fabric – a cotton, perhaps, or an *Indienne*, surely not silk, he'd never known such a precious material to be used for this sort of clothing, but the sensation on his skin was just like what you get with silk, warm and ethereal – and which came halfway down his thighs. He felt embarrassingly quite naked under it, but dared not check.

They walked cautiously along a white corridor, floor, walls, ceiling, all clad – it seemed to him – in foam padding, which erased the noise of their progress and made the walking both delicate and soft. After about a hundred yards, the Psychologist opened a door on his left. He placed the Investigator on a swivel chair and took a stool on castors for himself, with quite a high seat, metal, shaped like a tractor seat, one of those that hairdressers use to move around their clients, and came closer to the Investigator.

There was nothing interesting about the décor of the office, at least not enough to linger any time to describe it, but all the same, one thing leapt out to the Investigator's eyes: the immense portrait of the Old Man – face, clothes and pose identical to the photographs on the key-ring, in the hotel bedroom, in the Manager's office. Without understanding why, this terrified him, which did not escape the Psychologist's notice.

"Why are you looking at that wall?"

The Investigator, in a panic, could not tear himself away from the Old Man's smile, from his eyelids, which drooped down with just the same curve as his moustache, from the brightness – mocking? cheerful? kindly? appalling? – which burned in his eyes, from his spotted, wrinkled hands, streaked with cracks, hands that were a condensed signal of his advanced age, from his clothes that made you want to stroke them, against which you might have tried to snuggle up, to fall asleep in order to find forgiveness for your mistakes, your lies, your minor and major sins.

"That man . . ."

"A man? Tell me about him . . ." said the Psychologist, who had also just looked over at the wall.

"Excuse me?"

"You were saying something about a man, who is he?"

"I don't know . . . I don't know . . . I'm unsure."

"If it helps to reassure you, we all are."

"Is he the Founder?" the Investigator ventured.

The Psychologist rolled his stool, moving sideways like a crab, to position himself in front of the Investigator.

"The Founder?" he said, puzzled.

"Yes, the Founder."

The Psychologist seemed to hesitate, made as if to say something, changed his mind, then shrugged.

"If you like! Well, now, if you agree, I'd like us to come on to you. What is it that brings you here?"

The Investigator would gladly have crunched through one or two yellow and blue pills from his friend the Policeman, but the tube, like his telephone with the flat battery, had stayed behind in his raincoat and in any case it was empty. And besides, where were his clothes, then? He wasn't really at all sorry for their loss, the hospital gown he was wearing being far more pleasant and on the whole very practical, becoming, thin and supple as a second skin.

Forgetting all about his headache and gathering up his ideas, he then set about giving the Psychologist a summary of his situation, he went back over his arrival in the Town, insisted several times on his position and on his mission, described his wandering through the streets, the feeling of being lost, manipulated, the strangeness of the Hotel, the treatment that had varied from one morning to the next, the behaviour of the Policeman, first hostile and then friendly, that of the Giantess, he spoke of the streets deserted at night, the feeling of abandonment, of isolation, of the gigantism of The Firm that took in the whole Town, indeed the visible world, of the Crowd that poured through during the day, everywhere, and which prevented the slightest movement, the smallest initiative of personal displacement, unless you're a policeman, in which case the Crowd becomes a flock of sheep that a symbolic cudgel blow, a raised hand, a staring eye, was enough to bring into line, of the hostility of the sandwich machines, of the Exceptional Authorisation, of the Manager's failed jump onto his desk, of the Guide who was also the Watchman, of room 93 that he had methodically ransacked, of the Tourists, of The Displaced, of the inconstancy of the meteorology and the inability of Architects to design staircases with regular steps.

"Are you done?" the Psychologist asked.

"Yes, I think so – in any case, for now, I can't think of anything to add."

He had been talking for nearly an hour. It had done him good. He felt the Psychologist understood him. The man got up from his stool on castors to go and sit behind the desk. From one of the drawers he took an index card, a promotional ball-point pen on which the Investigator thought he recognised the image of the Old Man, but reproduced so small that he wouldn't have bet his life on it, then scribbled three words he wasn't able to read.

"Your name, please?" The Psychologist still had his head lowered, no doubt telling himself that the answer would come so quickly that it would be pointless for him to raise his head and look at his interlocutor.

"My name?"

"Yes."

The Psychologist still had his head lowered, the pen ready to write the Investigator's name, its tip suspended two centimetres above the paper.

"My name . . . my name . . . ?" stammered the Investigator, who was making a huge effort, but trying to hide it behind a smile which in spite of himself was turning into a grimace.

Slowly the Psychologist lifted his gaze and looked at him, his face betraying no emotion at all, not even the smallest thought going in one direction or the contrary. In other words, it was impossible to know just at that moment what the Psychologist thought about the Investigator, about the Investigator's hesitation in giving his name. Just the fact of his having looked up, that is, having traded a banal attitude for another that was slightly less so, which testified to an attention that was more sustained – more curious? – indicated that the time the Investigator took in replying revealed in his opinion – an opinion that was wrapped up with his status as a clinician, sustained by his knowledge and his already extensive professional experience, being no longer in the first flush of youth – an imperceptible break with normality.

Meanwhile, the Investigator was losing his footing. He was stepping onto quicksand. He had always doubted its existence. For a long time he had classified it as belonging in the same wardrobe that contained Aladdin's lamp, flying carpets, the tales of Scheherazade, Sinbad's Cyclops. He had heard of them, but no more than that. Legends and fables had never interested him. He did without. He left all that to children. He was wrong.

"You don't recall your name?"

# 36

THE INVESTIGATOR BURST OUT LAUGHING. A BIG LAUGH, LONG and flexible, which he stretched out as far as he could, hoping the Psychologist would be contaminated by this slightly fake good mood and would join him in this joyful change of tone. But the longer the laugh lasted, the more artificial this made it, the more the Investigator did his best to keep it going, to infuse it with new variations, and the more the Psychologist's face hardened, changed to a dull, extinguished surface, cold as a rock, impenetrable as granite.

He put his pen down on the piece of paper. The Investigator stopped laughing then. He knew he had lost. His thoughts began to run around his head, in every direction, like creatures held captive in a circular room and who hurtle around, rush at the walls, crash into them, bounce back, cry out, injure themselves, call out, beg, for someone to free them, or at least to answer them. He was searching. He was searching for his name. The name that was written on his I.D. papers. A simple movement was all it would have taken him, a glance at the plastic card which bore his photograph and on which his name was printed. Could it be that he'd forgotten his own name?

Was that one of the consequences of his accident against the wall? No-one forgets their own name! He must have said it a dozen times since he'd arrived in the Town. Surely! He thought about this, went back over all the meetings he had had, there weren't all that many of them, and tried to remember how he had addressed his inter-locutors: "I am the Investigator." "Hello, I'm the Investigator." "Allow me to introduce myself, I am the Investigator." The phrases linked onto one another, identical or almost identical. The Investigator remembered that he always defined himself as being the Investigator, which indeed he was. But not with a name. No name. Ever.

"I am the Investigator," he said to the Psychologist at last, shrugging his shoulders up and immediately dropping them down again, and in doing so apologising for this evidence that he was giving.

The Psychologist got up and went back to sit on the mobile stool. He slid it over to be as close as possible to the Investigator. The hardness of his face softened. His tone of voice went back to being flowing and smooth:

"Were you aware that you have only spoken in terms of functions since the start of our interview? You are the Investigator, you refer to the Policeman, the Guide, the Watchman, the Waiter, the Guard, the Manager, the Sentry, the Founder. You never use proper names, not for yourself nor for anyone else. Occasionally you kit yourself out with a number – you're 14, you're 93 – but that comes to the same thing. Reply to this simple question – what am I to you?"

"You're the Psychologist . . . Well, after all, my good man, isn't that what you told me?"

"No, I told you I was a psychologist, I didn't tell you I was the Psychologist. Moreover, you might have noticed, I am a woman, and you call me your 'good man', which confirms my analysis. You deny any humanity, in yourself or around you. You look at mankind and the world as an impersonal, asexual system of functions, of cogs, a great mechanism with no intelligence in which these functions and these cogs operate and interact in order to make it work. When you refer to a group of people *en masse*, it is vague and boundless, you talk of The Firm, the Crowd, the Tourists, The Displaced, nebulous entities where it's not clear whether they are to be taken literally or metaphorically."

"There's the Giantess!" the Investigator exclaimed, as if – filled with hope – he had discovered the blessed formula for an S.O.S. just when he felt that his ship was already almost entirely submerged.

"The Giantess," the Psychologist continued, smiling one of those smiles given to people who have trouble understanding something even when all the elements to do so have been provided to them. "The Giantess is also the Mother, too, your Mother, full stop. You could just as easily have said 'the Woman'. There too we have a function, and the exaggeration of the function that we can read in your use of the term 'Giantess' simply reflects the crushing you seem to feel when faced with the feminine, perhaps also the fantasy of being dominated by it, enveloped by it, of returning via a kind of reverse labour back into the great, first, ancestral uterus, in order to run away from a world in which you struggle to earn your place, or to keep it."

The Giantess – his Mother! His Mother in the uterus to which he dreams of returning. This woman was crazy! As evidence of this, the Investigator wasn't even able to recall his Mother's face.

"This, moreover, is doubtless why you wear women's undergarments?"

"Excuse me?"

The Psychologist rolled his stool over to a little piece of furniture where he opened a drawer, put in his hand and took out the pink knickers trimmed in black lace, which he waved in the air for a few seconds, before dropping them back in the drawer, flicking it closed again.

"I can explain everything . . ." the Investigator stammered, humiliated.

"I'm not asking you for any explanation. I'm not the Policeman, to use your terminology. It's up to me to provide explanations, that's what I'm paid for, not you. As someone with such respect for functions, please don't get them mixed up; tell me instead about this famous Investigation. Who commissioned you?"

"The Head of Department," the Investigator answered quickly, glad to forget the little pair of knickers in the drawer.

"Yet again you give a function. What is his name?"

"I don't know. I don't know anything! Between us we always call him the Head of Department. He's the Head of Department, that's all there is to it."

"When you say *between us*, who are you thinking of?"

"Well, the other Investigators."

"There are a lot of you?"

"Yes."

"How many?"

"I really don't know! Five, six, ten, hundreds, more than that, I don't know anything, the Head of Department is the one who knows. It's not for me to know!"

"And if I ask you the name of any of these other investigators, you'd tell me . . ."

". . . that I don't know, I don't run into them very often, I don't speak to them, I focus on my Investigations."

The conversation was becoming torture. The Investigator was getting entangled in his answers which weren't answers at all, and he was aware of this, which had the effect of making him even more fragile, and, to cap it all, he saw the look in the Psychologist's eye change, and he read in that change the progressive transformation that occurs in the mind of a professional: he was gradually stopping thinking of him as a being quite close to himself, evolving within a relative kind of normality, subject to certain perversions and faults, no doubt, but which were on the whole socially and humanly acceptable, and he began to comprehend within all his difference, which was becoming gradually clearer, a difference that was clearly pathological, monstrous, a special case the study of which would prove to be if not thrilling then at least altogether original.

"And this Investigation, then, its purpose was . . . ?" continued the Psychologist, leaving the words floating in the air, hanging there.

"The Suicides."

"The Suicides?"

"Yes, the epidemic of Suicides that has hit The Firm over several months."

"I wasn't aware of that, and if anyone should have been aware of such a thing it would certainly be me. Do you have proof of what you're suggesting?"

"My Head of Department isn't in the habit of joking, he can't stand wasting his time or that of his subordinates. I imagine that if he sent me to this town, to the heart of The Firm, to carry out an Investigation on the wave of Suicides, it's because such a wave exists. And what is more, even though this might make you smile, but given where I've come to I no longer have anything to lose, in any case I can hardly lose face now, I met the Suicides in a dream, and I was able to speak to them, just after I went into the wall. And I can assure you that the dream was far more real and far more eloquent than most of the allegedly real facts that I've experienced in this parody of reality since I got off the train!"

The Psychologist sighed deeply, smiled, lifted his arms right up and then let them fall back onto his lap.

"Naturally!"

He put his right hand on the Investigator's shoulder, stroking this sagging, flabby shoulder slightly, a shoulder which one might think didn't have a bone to hold it up, made up only of fat and wasted muscles, part of a mistreated body that hadn't eaten a thing in three days.

"You've convinced me," the Psychologist said. "I'm going to set everything in progress so that you can carry out your Investigation successfully."

He returned to his desk and wrote out a long message. "A sort of passport which will open doors for you," he added, throwing the occasional kindly glance over towards the Investigator.

Reassured now, the Investigator was finally able to relax. He was, he thought, finally just a hair's breadth away from starting on his mission for good. He felt confident, and this feeling wasn't only the result of the pleasant material his thin hospital gown was made of, over which he ran his fingers, one way then the other, in a slow, stroking motion, nor even due to the Policeman's medication. This temporary fragment of happiness was born from the conclusion he had reached: you should always put all your cards on the table, he said to himself, that's the only way to get taken seriously in life, even if the cards sometimes show incongruous figures, blind kings, one-eyed jacks, doubtful queens, which could throw even the most robust of us and make us question the hand we're holding. But fortunately there are certain individuals who look beyond appearances. And the Investigator, considering all this, wondered at the features of the Psychologist who was leaning over his desk, as one does wonder at those women and men who comfort us in our existence.

## 37

THE PSYCHOLOGIST HAD SEALED THE ENVELOPE, AND IT WOULD not have occurred to the Investigator to open it to read what it said inside, as the name the Psychologist had written on the envelope was enough both to comfort him and to prohibit him. There in capital letters, drawn by a hand that was sure of itself, that brooked no dissent and contained no hesitation in it, were the words: "FOR THE FOUNDER".

The Investigator was sitting in a sort of waiting room where the Psychologist had led him, very kindly helping him to walk there, as though he were very sick, while in fact, if you excepted the pain that still bored into his head but which was all the same beginning to fade, his general condition seemed to him to be rather satisfactory. His hunger was not troubling him, and he wasn't even thirsty.

"Make yourself comfortable," the Psychologist had told him, "I'll go and fetch, I'll go and fetch . . . um, what can I call them that you'll like . . . ?" He had hesitated a moment, his left index finger on his lips, looking at the Investigator. ". . . The Escorts. Does that work for you, 'Escorts'?"

"Escorts? That's perfect!" the Investigator had seen fit to reply, the very name of "Escort" resonating reassuringly in his mind.

"They will take you to the . . . Founder. I'm sure he will be very happy to meet you."

The Investigator had thanked him, then the Psychologist had left, leaving him in the company of a common evergreen plant in a pot, a water-cooler (empty) and a pile of magazines that had been left on a low table. The lighting in the room was violently bright, and there were no windows. Just like the Psychologist's office, as well as the corridors they'd walked, it was white, entirely white, the floor and walls covered in that material that was both smooth and soft and which absorbed shocks as well as sounds.

All of a sudden, as he looked at the floor and the walls, the violently bright light, remembering the Psychologist's comments, the way he'd looked at him, listened to him, the Investigator felt an insidious unease which at first he ignored. It was like an idea scratching at a distant door, the door of a residence made up of dozens of rooms and dozens of doors. Or, to record another image that occurred to the Investigator, as though someone in the fourth-floor room of a building senses that somebody has lightly rung the bell at the front gate, but such a quick, fleeting ring that he doesn't altogether know whether he heard the bell or whether he dreamed it. In any case, his perception of things is changed by it, and he's no longer the same as he was before that real or hypothetical doorbell ring, and his future actions will one way or another be influenced by what he heard or thought he heard.

Certainly, there was too much whiteness making up this

Waiting Room. Much too much whiteness. A world of whiteness, in which moreover the shapes tended to disappear as well as the objects, which were also white, like the chair on which he was sitting, the low table with the magazines on it, the water-cooler, the pot holding the evergreen, which was only green in name as it, too, was totally white, white leaves and stalks that looked like a large bleached-out fern. After all, the Investigator said to himself, having been brought up short a moment by the strangeness of the plant, there are plenty of albino rabbits, why not ferns? And he was carried away by this whiteness spread around him in the smallest details and the smallest objects in this room, the way a pure, solidified snow creates an impression of serene, rigorous and simple beauty that has the benefit of resting the eyes and the mind.

The Investigator shut his eyes. Passed over from white to black. He stayed like this, eyelids closed, for some time, trying to cut himself off from the surrounding whiteness he sensed might perhaps absorb him, dissolve him, make him disappear, and he was letting himself go. He forced himself not to think about it too much. Not to let himself go, exactly. To be the Investigator. Not to forget to be that. To remain that. To stay that, at any cost.

He no longer got surprised by or worn down by the situations he'd been through in the last few days. After all, life is made up of these impossible, inexplicable moments, which we struggle to interpret, and which might not mean anything else at all. It's just a biological chaos we try to organise and to justify. But when for some reason or other the organisation is somehow lacking, whether it's because it is worn down, inappropriate, obsolete, whether it's because whoever is in charge of it has resigned, man finds himself facing events, emotions, questions, deadlocks and moments of illumination heaped on top of one another like differently sized blocks of ice swept away by mighty avalanches and set down in a jagged-edged pyramid that teeters in an unstable equilibrium on the brink of a great precipice.

The Investigator reopened his eyes and focused on what he was holding in his hands: the envelope that carried the words "FOR THE FOUNDER". This was something tangible, indubitable. The power of the object, of the felt, existing object, whose matter was in contact with the cells of his skin, the nerve endings implanted there and which transmitted the proof of the object's reality to the Investigator's consciousness in a millionth of a second. It had nothing to do with this business of a doorbell being rung or not! But why was he suddenly thinking about a doorbell ringing?

He banished this thought and picked up one of the magazines. Its glossy cover had no title and no photograph: it was blank, white. He opened it, leafed through it, getting more and more nervous. Nothing. Every one of the pages was equally milky-white. He picked up a second magazine, then a third, then a fourth, he leafed through them all. None of them had a single character printed in it, a single illustration, or photograph or even the smallest drawing! They were all in different formats, different in thickness or the quality of their paper, but they were also all identical, because they contained nothing! They were no more than collections of sheets of paper of constant, uniform, monotonous whiteness. But what most troubled the Investigator, what made him shudder and distressed him, was that these magazines had been leafed through, by dozens, hundreds of fingers, as the bottom corners of the pages bore witness, dog-eared, crumpled, slightly soiled with an ivory sheen. They had been leafed through, or they had been read . . . If his eyes weren't able to make anything out, was that really the same for everyone? Could he have fallen victim to a partial or selective blindness, because would anyone really have thought to print, distribute, create, imagine, white magazines? Magazines that contained nothing? Nothing at all? And could people – people without jobs? without intelligence? people with such highly conditioned behaviour? – have read them just the same, spent their time running their eyes over pages stripped of any information, any text, any photography? To what benefit? Yes, for what purpose would people spend their time reading something that does not exist?

The Investigator was feeling feverish again, nervous, unsettled. He threw the last magazine he was holding onto the floor, and picked up the envelope from the Psychologist that he had wedged under his thigh.

"FOR THE FOUNDER". He reread the addressee three times. If he was reading it, it was because he was able to read it. Which meant that those three words existed on the envelope. Which meant that he could read them and hadn't suddenly – from the crash against the wall or the abuse of medication – lost the capacity to see hand-written or printed characters. He wanted to clear things up in his mind, he didn't think about it, and with a clumsy, rough gesture tore the envelope to extract the message that the Psychologist had written.

It was a sheet of creamy-white paper, folded carefully in four – it was still possible to make out the marks of the Psychologist's nails that had painstakingly creased the edges. The Investigator unfolded the piece of paper, looked at it, turned it over, turned it over again, with increasingly brutal about-turns in his trembling fingers: the piece of paper was blank, white, dramatically white, irremediably white.

It bore no trace of any ink, and not a word.

Nothing.

It was immaculate.

# 38

IN MANY WARS AND OTHER LESS EXTREME CIRCUMSTANCES, MEN'S capacity for resistance has been tested by submitting them to physical or mental challenges whose refinement over the centuries has done nothing to belie humanity's ability to excel itself in the imagination and the execution of horror.

From a simple drop of water falling repeatedly onto the forehead of a condemned man, to the torture of the choke pear, to that of Spanish boots, of the breaking wheel, of quartering, of inoculating a healthy limb with gangrene, of the forced insertion of living rats into the vagina of a torture victim, of the peremptory amputation of all four limbs, of the sun being given the responsibility of browning the skull of a naked man almost completely buried in the sands of the desert, of the hundred scraps of flesh taken slowly with a knife from a living body, from the bathtub of freezing water into which a child is submerged in order to measure the duration of his agony, to the use of electricity as a stimulus, to the spectacle inflicted on a man forced to watch his wife, his daughter and son executed with a bullet in the back of the neck, to the traditional and persistent use of rape, of disembowelling, of prolonged confinement in extreme conditions, of forced nudity as an attempt at humiliation, of gradual throat-slitting with a rusty, deliberately unsharpened blade, of perpetual solitude in the belief that it leads to the idea in the mind of the person being mistreated that he alone is to blame for his situation and for all the tortures inflicted on him, man is found to be not the wolf that he is said to be to other men, which is offensive to wolves which really are civilised, socialised creatures, but more precisely the anti-man, in the way physicists speak of anti-matter.

So who wanted to destroy the Investigator? So who was so determined to grind him down like common grain from which the poor flour will be dispersed into the wind for ever? Who, and why? Because this was the conclusion he had reached in the sound-proof intimacy of the white room. This conclusion in the form of a double question. Far exceeding hunger and thirst, far beyond time whose flow he could not – or could no longer – quantify, understanding just how relative it turned out to be, far beyond pure questions of identity – who was he really? – the Investigator gradually felt the emptiness in which he was hovering and which made him up. Had he not himself become a matter in conflict with an expanding anti-matter? Was he not moving – quickly or slowly, it hardly mattered – towards the black hole that would swallow him up? Was there someone – but who? Who? – who wanted to confront him with a radical and definitive metaphorical insight into his life, into human life generally?

The Investigator was questioning his thoughts, questioning his faculty of thought. In the absence of any points of reference – how was it possible to grasp the whiteness, the magazines written in letters that have disappeared, or an evergreen that isn't? – he convinced himself that he wasn't altogether alive, and therefore wasn't altogether thinking.

"I am not thinking, they are thinking through me, or rather, they are thinking me. There's no possibility of my taking any initiative. I'm led to believe I have an Investigation to conduct. Actually I'm sure it's nothing. I am chucked around, messed about, crushed and then stroked, jostled over and got back up on my feet. I am moved and moved again, forbidden from crossing a road and then a path is opened for me, I'm smiled at, I'm embraced, I'm warmed up again only to be dashed the next moment against a wall. My brain is washed with great showers of rain and snow, cold and heat, I'm starved, deprived of drink, stuffed with food, made to vomit, humiliated by being made to wear any old kinds of clothing, I'm prevented from cleaning myself, shut away in a room, I'm listened to patiently only to be abandoned all the more quickly to my fate. What justification could be found for that?"

The Investigator would have paid dearly to be able to go backwards, to be at the heart of a reel of film being played in reverse, to beat a lengthy retreat, which would have brought him gradually back onto the running-board of the train, a little rectangle of metal openwork which he ought never to have stepped off, to be back in the carriage that he barely remembered, finding himself in the Head of Department's office at the moment when the other man spoke to him of his mission – what were the precise words he'd used? Hard to recall – in his apartment the morning he'd left, but he was so tired that he couldn't picture his apartment, he would have been unable to describe it, even to give its exact address, still less the storey number or the arrangement of the furniture, how it was floored – wall-to-wall carpet? tiling? parquet? – or the walls decorated – paint or wallpaper?

At that exact moment, which it would still have been possible to date even if this hadn't been especially useful, he had another thought without any logical basis, a blaze which glowed brightly, but which was destined for an immediate death, as happens with large fireworks in the dark summer night sky: he had the sense that all the places he'd been through, all the awkward streets, the long walls, the buildings he'd seen, the bar from the first day, the Hotel, even the Guardhouse, the glass cone with the Manager's office in it, maybe even the Psychologist's office had already ceased to exist – about which from one perspective he was correct – that they had never, in truth, existed except during the brief moment he had passed among them, and that this was so, too, for the people he'd encountered, who had also disappeared, extinguished at just the same time as the places he'd seen them living in had been extinguished, steeped in a lethargy with no return, made metaphorical in the Guide's Level 6 Hindrance, and that this universal disappearance – complete, irreversible – might perhaps have signalled the flaws in his memory, the exhausting of his intellectual and psychic faculties that no longer allowed him to retain anything, and that he was now getting ready to become a being who, simply, would no longer be, joining the destiny of all those other beings who one day end up dying, even if for the whole of the rest of their existence they never cease to call this implacable evidence into question.

At the same time, the thought of the destruction of his thought, the awareness that the white that surrounded him and which had contaminated the whole landscape, walls and furnishings, undoubtedly prefigured the greater, limitless white towards which he was progressing, this thought did prove that he was still, despite everything, thinking! And that the hope of remaining, of lasting longer, even if only a little longer, did exist. All the misadventures he had been through, the collision with the wall, the obsession with seeing the Founder's portrait everywhere he looked and the isolation in the whiteness, still had not destroyed him altogether. The Investigator was proving to be very robust, even within the very awareness of his own disappearance. But how painful it all was! He couldn't take any more of the mad race that was going on within the walls of his skull. And he was starting to feel cold. Very cold.

He was holding his too-light gown with both hands and trying to stretch it, to lengthen it, to stretch it out it so it would cover his body a bit more, but in distorting the material he only managed to tear it at his left shoulder, and it was at that moment, at the moment when he was doing that most human of gestures of clothing himself, that the walls and floor of the Waiting Room began to move, as though this movement had been synchronised with the tearing of the material that had caused a delicate unzipping noise, and a few seconds later, just as the trembling of the walls and the floor increased, a sudden metallic commotion burst into life, made up of the rattling of axles, of wheels, of things rubbing together, of crashing and banging, bringing to the Investigator's mind a very clear image of the train that had brought him to this town and whose dilapidation had rather surprised him, even if he hadn't taken much notice, yes, out of his memory came that train and many others, dozens, hundreds, thousands of trains that combined all their engines and their carriages filled with resigned travellers, all of them with more or less the same characteristics as the Investigator, all of them tossed around, powerless, surprised, and who made up, quite in spite of themselves, the interminable, stunned parade of human History.

The pitching grew as the din grew, while whistlings, hammerings, perhaps voices, too, but he wasn't quite sure, seemed to be perspiring from the padded walls, literally perspiring, the voices transforming into drops of sweat, of oily, sticky liquid, a kind of resin that seeped from outside to fill the white walls, to penetrate them, pass through them and saturate the room.

The Investigator would have liked to rip out his ears so he wouldn't hear any more, to rip out his eyes so he wouldn't see any more, rip out his soul so as not to continue to suffer this nightmare, but he could do none of these things. The room tumbled in every direction, conflicting forces crushing him, wringing him out, making him fly up to the ceiling, the ceiling which was now transformed into the floor, then into a side wall, then back to a ceiling only to become – brutally – the floor again. The Investigator felt no physical pain, even if he didn't stop bumping into things. Everything was soft. The shocks were muffled and when some object, a low table, chair, magazine, potted evergreen plant which was white, crashed into him, it seemed to him as though nothing was happening and the object was simply passing through him without any injury or harm. He thought about those men whom the Species had been regularly sending out into space for several decades in order to explore its furthest reaches or to take – ludicrously, and very temporarily – possession of it. He remembered seeing them floating in the air in their cabin, spinning, sucking up liquids which hung suspended in droplets of different sizes and colours, playing with adjustable spanners which had become light as feathers, bowling balls that were now soap bubbles. He remembered their slow voices, blurred and corrupted by interference from the hundreds of thousands of kilometres they'd had to travel to get to Earth, and the slow-motion smile of these men locked into an enclosed space, far from the world, hurtling around in the universe at sidereal speeds, alone, without any real possibility of return, nor any desire to return. Yes, he remembered their smile, an eternal smile with nothing earthly or human about it any longer, detached as they were from the original blue globe that to them seemed to have the proportions of a distant toy ball.

Then he himself began to smile, and gave himself up.

# 39

FOR SEVERAL MINUTES THERE WAS A RAY OF LIGHT, WHITE, incandescent, striking the Investigator's left eyelid. Eventually he felt its heat and opened an eye, but closed it again right away, the brightness being such that it was not possible to look straight at it. He tried to open the other, but it was just as impossible. The light was far too violent. He moved his head a little, then his body, then half-opened his eyelids again. The light was sparing his eyes now and beating down on his neck. It was coming in through the door whose lock had given way.

The Investigator awoke all of a sudden, looked around him: the Waiting Room was upside-down: the furniture was on the ground, the chairs and the table smashed, the pallid plant lay in the debris of its pot, the magazines looked like the peelings of enormous, chlorotic tubers. He got up, patted down his body, expecting to see it collapse into a thousand and one pieces, but nothing of the sort happened. Only the hospital gown had been even more badly torn: it left two-thirds of his chest bare.

Slightly fearful, he pushed at the door, gently, and then, when nothing dreadful happened, smacked it hard against the wall outside. The sun poured in like water escaping from a valve that has been suddenly released. That light, so it was only the sun, the sun that was beating him so hard. A ball of fire with shifting outlines, pale yellow, hanging over the horizon, and he could not tell if it was moving away from that horizon or if it was about to dissolve into it. The Investigator held his hands over his eyes as a visor. Thus protected, he was gradually able to take the measure of the place he found himself.

It was a sort of vast, imprecise powdery landscape, flat without any protrusions, on which, in some arrangement that was not easy to understand, there were containers grouped here and there that looked like large caravans without wheels, some of them clad with steel or aluminium, rhomboid armour, incandescent with the reflection of the light, others beaten up, like big battered cardboard boxes, huts on construction sites, whose plasterboard, compressed-wood or light sheet-metal walls were staved in all over their surfaces. Occasionally a few of them were grouped together in perfect alignment, while others had been knocked askew, crammed together, others tipped over or lying on their side. There were some that were isolated, around which – without there being any mark on the ground to signal any sort of border, an enclosure or a bound-ary – the others had kept a sensible gap. There were some that made up groups where a hierarchy of size appeared to be in operation, or a hierarchy of scale, or materials, of good or bad condition. Some containers were brand new, as though they had come right off the assembly line, others, meanwhile, showed their decrepitude in the corrosion of their materials, the dirty marks that covered their ori-ginal surfaces or the liberties taken with geometry when assembling their sides.

The Investigator took a few steps forward. The heat was stifling, and the sun did not move. Nothing seemed to suggest its descent, nor its ascent either. It was a day in suspension, scorching, not an evening and not a morning, something distinguished not by its having a place in a conventional unfolding of time but by the immobility of its light and its heat. The whiteness of the ground, covered in an earth that looked like plaster, prevented the Investigator from being able to make out what was surrounding him. He managed to get to grips with the foreground, to isolate the dozens and dozens of containers that were positioned not too far from him, but beyond that, despite his best efforts, he was not able to see a thing, as everything disappeared into the tremulous float-ing of the air which expanded the atmosphere into moving, trans-lucent smoke, behind which the landscape collapsed into an elusive void.

The Firm, like the Town, could not be too far away. His journey in the container had not lasted long, at least that was his impression. But what did he really know?

He was almost naked, and yet his forehead and his body had become covered with sweat and he had only left the Waiting Room – he persisted in calling it that, the beaten-up prefab that lay there, its door open, three metres away from him, doubtless in order to persuade himself that everything would be getting back in order – a very short time beforehand, about twenty seconds at the most. He was experiencing a feeling of great lightness. His steps – he took a few – did not tire him in the least. Only the heat, and he had never before felt such a heat, made him unwell, as, besides roasting him, it also drew out a profuse sweat from his body that streamed down his legs, between his thighs, his back, on his chest, the back of his neck, his lower back, his forehead, ran uninterrupted and particularly into his eyes, flooding them, adding liquid blindness to the luminous blindness, which meant that in a sense while it was obvious that the Investigator was not able to see all that much, he was, in fact, able to see less and less.

With his arms and hands stretched out towards nothing, vainly expecting to block out a sun that got itself into everything, as though his limbs had become transparent, the Investigator sought some shade. But as he tried to walk in every direction, and in particular walking right round the Waiting Room, he was not able to find the least little bit, which defied all logic and all laws of physics, since if the sun was beating down on one wall, it could not be beating down on the one that was opposite it, given that the star was far from being at its highest point, settling for a sleepy position just a touch above the horizon, but the Investigator had ceased being surprised by anything at all.

He stopped, breathless, sat down on the ground, or rather kneeled, bent his body over, sank his head in his shoulders, curled in on himself as much as he could, put his two hands on the sides of his temples, shrunk to a shape resting on the ground, merely a shape, no different from a large stone, or a parcel that one might have wondered, if one had noticed it, what it contained. And what indeed did it contain, but a few dozen kilos of manhandled, burning flesh, inhabited by a soul that was battered about, unsure and worn out?

The Investigator had no more tears. Even if he had wanted to cry, he would have been unable to do so. All the water in his body was leaving as sweat. He moaned. Moaned again. Trying to bury his head further in his arms and into his torso to shield it from the sun. His moaning became a cry, low at first, relatively soundless, then it grew, roared, growled, hauling out the last jolts of an energy that was gradually disappearing, ending up with an explosion, a long bellow that was final, powerful, animalistic, which could have sent shivers up your spine if it had not been quite so hot.

It happens in zoos that the cries of large apes or peacocks wake up other species, and that then, in the very middle of the night or in the tranquil afternoon hours, when everything is asleep and there's nothing to lead you to expect it, a noisy protest is unleashed, a kind of living storm made up of hundreds of sounds and crushed-together voices that then form a thunder of noises, deep and high-pitched, bursts of whistling, guttural eruptions, yapping, hooting, growling, stamping, crashing against the cage bars, wire-netting being bashed about, barking, trumpeting, which electrifies a passer-by and plunges him into a nightmare all the greater because he cannot make out the precise origin of each of the sounds that stampede around him, bind him up tight, smother him and prevent him from escaping the increasingly agonising cacophony. The Investigator had not yet completely finished his howling when from most of the containers, gigantic, prefabricated boxes, mobile homes, lock-ups scattered around him, there rose up blows that were muffled or clearly audible, cries, groans, murmurs, voices, yes, there was no doubt that there were voices, human voices, in which it was possible to make out a tone of supplication without being able to understand the words, voices of ghosts or of men condemned, voices of the dying, voices of the excluded, a thousand years old, ancestral and yet at the same time appallingly present, voices that surrounded the Investigator and suffocated his own.

## 40

EVENTUALLY THE VOICES HAD FALLEN SILENT. GRADUALLY. ONE AT a time. In a progressive disappearance, as though a skilful finger, somewhere, acting in the name of a higher will, had slid down a button that regulated their intensity. The Investigator could not get over it. He turned around and around until he made himself dizzy, and eventually stopped, reeling.

"Is anyone there?" he ventured after a few seconds.

"Over here!"

"Here!"

"Me!"

"Hello!"

"Here I am . . .!"

"Me! Me!"

At varying volumes bearing witness to their distances, but also to the reserves of energy that animated them, the voices were heard once again, isolated at first and then mixed together, muddled, melted into one another, making an unbearable jumble that seemed to saturate the air, filling it up like a fog or a drizzle.

The Investigator ran over to the closest container, knocked

on the wall. Bangs from inside answered him at once.

"Who are you?" the Investigator asked, pressing his ear to the wall.

"Open up for me, for pity's sake, open up . . . I can't take it anymore . . ." the muffled voice inside the container replied.

"But who are you?" the Investigator asked again.

"I'm . . . I'm . . ."

The voice faltered, broke off. The Investigator even thought he could hear sobbing.

"But just tell me who you are!"

"I was . . . I was . . . the Investigator."

The Investigator leapt back as though burned. His heart went wild.

"Please don't go, don't leave me . . . please . . ."

The Investigator's chest clenched under a violent pressure. His heart was beating uncontrollably and entirely at random, with unexpected accelerations followed by abrupt slowing-down. He held his hand on it, trying to calm it, to reassure it as though he were dealing with an animal that had caught its paw in a snare, and which, rather than trying to cut through the bond with its teeth, was going against all logic by trying to gnaw at his paw to free it. It did him good. With the back of one hand he wiped away the sweat that did not stop gushing down his forehead and made him feel as though he were dissolving.

He examined the container.

It was one of more recent-looking ones, one of the newest. The film of dust that covered it was fine and translucent. Careful to make as little noise as possible, he began to walk around it in order to locate the door.

"I can hear you, you know, you're moving about . . ."

The Investigator continued his progress, trying not to worry about the voice that had spoken these words so desperately. He moved on tiptoes, trying to keep light on his feet. He passed the corner of the container, inspected the wall that he came to, didn't see a door, and went on.

"Why don't you answer me . . . ?"

The Investigator continued his inspection. He went round the next corner. The shorter wall appeared. Still nothing. No door.

". . . just one word . . . please, I know you're still there . . . I know it . . ."

There was only one wall left. Just one. The Investigator sped up. The container man could hear him. There was no longer any point being careful as he walked. And anyway, why did he feel such dread? The man didn't seem aggressive, and he was shut in. The Investigator was about to pass the final corner, but he slowed down. Or rather, his body slowed down, even before his thoughts had told it to. What was it he feared, exactly? What was he afraid of? What imminent discovery was paralysing him at this moment? He knew, but he didn't dare admit it. The three walls of the container that he'd looked at did not include a single door, a single opening. This meant, then, that the door was to be found in the fourth wall. He just had to step round the corner to confirm that. And yet, he didn't do it. He didn't dare to do it. He didn't dare, because, deep down, he was certain that that fourth wall didn't include a single door, a single window, even if this made no sense.

The Investigator allowed himself to slide down to the ground, and sat down, his back against the container. He would prefer not to check. He would prefer to cling to uncertainty. Only uncertainty, he said to himself, would allow him to hang on longer, just a little longer. For it had to be one of two things: either the fourth wall of the container housed a door, or it did not house a door. If his eyes saw the door, all would be well. But if his eyes confirmed the absence of a door, there would be nothing left for him but to drown in his madness or to be cooked by this wretched sun which was just there, still in the same place, making its heat stream down onto the bare earth. The Investigator preferred not to know and to cling to the possibility, the slim possibility, that he was still in a world in which enclosed places could only contain a thing, something, someone, an evergreen plant albeit a bleached-out one, if they had some opening through which that thing had got in.

"You're still there, aren't you . . . ?"

The voice in the container was very close. It reverberated into the Investigator's back. The man must have had his mouth stuck right up against the wall. His words entered the Investigator's body, with a sort of tickling sensation.

"Answer me . . ."

"Who are you?" the Investigator asked again.

"I've told you already, I'm the Investigator."

"But I'm the Investigator!"

There was a silence, then he thought he heard a sigh.

"If you say so . . . But in any case we all are, more or less . . ."

"I don't understand."

"Think whatever you like . . . I'm not going to fight, I no longer have the strength . . . This whole thing has wiped me out . . . Can you help me get out of here, please?"

"I'm afraid not. Your box seems to be hermetically sealed."

"A box? But they asked me to stay in the Waiting Room . . ."

The Investigator moved away from the wall a little, looked at the container again.

"I'm calling it a box for brevity's sake, you're actually imprisoned in a sort of prefabricated building that's been dumped in the middle of nowhere."

"Nowhere . . ."

The voice fell silent. The Investigator didn't know what to do. On the other side of the wall, he could sense a man who, with perhaps just a few discrepancies, had no doubt been through similar events to those that he'd faced himself.

"It's cold, it's so cold . . ." the voice murmured.

"What are you talking about?" asked the astonished Investigator, whose body was visibly melting, dissolving into liquid, into water, into sweat. "I haven't got anything covering my skin and I'm still too hot. It's like the sun is just hanging in the sky. It doesn't move, not even a millimetre. There are no clouds, and when a little breeze picks up it's to pour waves of burning dust into this heat!"

"You're so lucky . . . I've been trying to curl up in my clothes, I'm numb with cold. There are ice crystals everywhere, on my beard, my hands, on the walls, on the low table, even on the evergreen in the pot. What's more, it does look as though it's completely white, I can't feel my feet or my hands anymore, I think they're frozen, I think they're already dead . . ."

The container didn't look like a cold storage room, and its outer walls, made of plywood, covered in a coat of beige paint, were hot to the touch. Was this voice telling the truth? Was this not yet another of those tests he was being made to undergo?

"What Investigation are you carrying out?" asked the Investigator.

"I was meant to . . . I was meant to . . . Oh, what's the use in explaining it to you . . ."

The voice had lost all its strength. The Investigator had to press his ear as close as he could against the wall to hear it.

"Were you conducting an enquiry at the heart of The Firm, about the Suicides?" the Investigator tried again.

"The Firm . . . ? The Suicides . . . ? No . . . no . . . I was asked to . . . Well, I was supposed to try and . . . explain . . . the decreased motivation in the Group . . . So cold . . . cold . . . My lips are frozen, too, my eyes, I can't see anymore . . ."

"But what Group? What are you talking about?"

"The Group . . . the Group . . ."

"A Group that's a part of The Firm?"

"The Firm . . . ?"

"Oh, but really," the Investigator said, beginning to get annoyed, "do make an effort. If you're where you are, there's surely a reason for it, for God's sake! You don't end up where you are without a reason, the Group you're talking about must surely be in The Firm. Answer me!"

"Group . . . motivation . . . tongue . . . frozen . . . Firm . . . can't now . . . can't now . . ."

"Answer me!"

". . . anymore . . ."

The Investigator started yelling, beating both his hands against the walls of the box, dropping the confessional tone he had previously been using. Then there arose again – coming from dozens, hundreds, thousands of walled-in voices – even more than that? How could he know? – an outburst of shouts and cries of rage, groans, tragic appeals, complaints, prayers, entreaties that gave the Investigator the sense that he was being scratched from all directions, that people were clinging to him like castaways clinging to a poor rowing boat they know full well cannot save them all, but who nonetheless continue to do it with the sole, selfish aim of making it sink, so that it will save no-one, unconsciously preferring the death of everyone to one person's survival.

The Investigator couldn't find any escape from it all but to block his ears and close his eyes.

## 41

VERY OFTEN WE TRY TO COMPREHEND WHAT ELUDES US USING our own terms and concepts. Ever since man differentiated himself from other species, he hasn't stopped measuring the universe and the laws that govern it by reference to his thinking and the thoughts that it produces, while never acknowledging that part of his approach is ineffective. Yet he is well aware, for example, that a sieve is unsuitable for collecting water. So why, then, does he consistently deceive himself into believing that his mind can understand everything and grasp everything? Why does he not realise rather that his mind is a prosaic sieve, that is, a utensil that is undeniably effective in certain circumstances, for specific actions, and in certain situations, but that it is of no use at all in others, because it is not made for that, because it has holes in it, because so many elements pass through it without it managing to hold them or enable their examination even if only for a few seconds.

Was it because of the infinite heat? Was it because he couldn't stop sweating, oozing, disappearing into his own humours? Was it because he was thirsty without even being fully aware of it, that the Investigator was starting to think about human imperfection, about liquids and a sieve?

Silence again. His eyes were still closed. His hands had long ago dropped down the sides of his body. The voices had fallen silent. The only sounds that came to his ears were the moanings of the wind as it played between the containers. He suddenly felt a little less hot, just as the darkness beyond his closed eyelids turned darker still.

A shadow.

It had to be a shadow, a thick cloud masking the sun, unless the sun itself had finally decided to drop.

He opened his eyes. There was a man standing in front of him, whom he could only see in silhouette and whose large, fat body was casting a shadow over him. The man seemed vast. He wasn't a cloud. In his right hand he was holding what looked like a broom handle.

"Where have you got out from?" asked the Shadow. It was an old man's voice – heavy, deep, a little hoarse, but which despite its roughness had kept a lively, slightly ironic freshness to it. The other voices, the ones from the containers, launched back into their wailing.

"WE WILL HAVE SILENCE!" shouted the Shadow, and it was immediately quiet. The Investigator couldn't believe it. Who could he be, this shadow, to have such brutal, unquestionable authority over all these walled-in people?

"I asked you a question," the Shadow said.

"The Waiting Room. I was in the Waiting Room, over there . . ."

the Investigator replied slowly, leaning on the wall of the container to stand himself up, which he managed to do with considerable difficulty. The Shadow moved. His head turned towards where the Investigator had gestured. For a moment he looked at the disembowelled prefab, its door open, out of which the Investigator had come. The Investigator himself had the sun in his eyes again, that wretched sun which had not moved an inch and which was blinding him.

"You can't see a thing," the Shadow said. "Wait, I'll fix that."

The Investigator felt a hand touch him and tear away what was left of his gown. At once he tried to hide his crotch, but the cavernous voice pre-empted his movement: "You aren't going to start all that old business again . . . What good will it do you? No-one here can see you, apart from me and I'm in the same state as you." The Investigator heard the Shadow tear his gown into several pieces, then his hands, his old hands with their long gnarled fingers, brushed past his face and bound strips around his eyes, in a number of layers, delicately, holding the fabric and knotting it behind his head, but not too tightly in order to allow his eyelids complete freedom of movement.

"There. Done. You can open them now."

The world now appeared to the Investigator through this orangey gauze that hitherto had served as his clothing. The sun was no more than a straw-coloured ball and the ground had lost some of its blinding whiteness. Here and there he could make out darker blocks: they were the unequal masses of the various containers. The plain – flat, with no contours, no protrusions – was covered with them as far as the eye could see – there weren't dozens of them, nor even hundreds as he'd thought at first, but thousands, tens of thousands! – and the sight of this infinity brought a sweet bile to his dry mouth. He thought he was about to throw up. But what could he have thrown up?

In each of these boxes, he said to himself, there's a man, a man like him, who had been messed about, manhandled, who had been allowed to hope, led to believe he had a mission to carry out, a role to play, some place to exist, who had been made an ass of, humiliated, belittled, who had been shown the fragility of his condition, of his memories and his certainties, perhaps an Investigator or a man who claimed to be one, a man who was now shouting and beating against the walls without there being anyone to come to his help. A man who could have been him, if only his own box, being less solid or more ill-treated, hadn't opened.

He who had so long believed himself unique was now weighing up the significance of his mistake, and it terrorised him.

"Much better, isn't it?"

The Investigator jumped. He had almost forgotten the Shadow.

"In this place you blindfold your eyes so that you're able to see."

The Shadow was coming into focus, as sometimes a mirage can do. The Investigator could make out his features and the outlines of his body. He was indeed an old man, with a distended belly that fell in several folds and hid his genitals. The skin on his thighs reminded him of that on ancient animals of long-vanished species, and his sagging chest looked like the withered breasts of an old wet-nurse. His shoulders were drooping, too, soft, rounded, receding lines that connected to obese arms on which the skin hung like torn spiders' webs. But when the Investigator looked up at his face, he got such a shock that he thought the ground was disappearing beneath his feet and he would have fallen if the Shadow had not taken hold of him with his right hand, his left still gripping the broom handle which seemed to serve him as both walking-stick and sceptre: the high forehead on which a web of wrinkles sketched out deltas and streams, those saggy jowls, that dimpled chin, those ears behind which a silvery mane of hair cascaded down in grey waves, that thick moustache whose heavy tips fell down either side of a mouth with chapped lips, the Investigator had looked at them many times, and even though he couldn't make out the expression which was almost completely hidden behind the blindfold, he did have to accept this staggering piece of evidence:

"The Founder! You're the Founder . . ." he managed to say, as he felt waves of electricity run through his body.

"The Founder . . ." the Shadow repeated.

He seemed to reflect a moment, then shrugged.

"If it makes you happy . . . I'm not in the habit of being contrary. On the other hand, what I'm quite sure, is that you, you are the first man."

"The First Man? . . ."

"Yes, the first to come out of one of these boxes. No-one has ever been lucky like you before. But don't kid yourself, you are only enjoying a brief reprieve. You'll end up like the others. Being outside or inside, it doesn't change a thing. That's how this particular ship works. Everyone's inside, one way or another."

The Shadow gave the container another big slap, which drew no response from inside.

"You see? It's all over for him. No reaction anymore. He must have given up the ghost. These lock-ups are so well devised and so well sealed that it's pointless trying to open them. I've tried to do it often – yes, for the sake of humanity, and also to put a dent in my boredom. I gave up trying after I'd broken three nails and sprained my wrist."

The Shadow mimicked the action to the word, rubbing his forearm as though the reference to the incident had reawakened the pain.

"What's odd is discovering that misfortune is a weight that ultimately gets quite light the more extreme it becomes or the more it proliferates. Seeing a man die before one's eyes is extremely unpleasant. Almost unbearable. Seeing or hearing millions of them dying dilutes the horror, and the compassion. You're quickly surprised at how you no longer feel much. Numbers are the enemy of emotion. So who has ever felt the suffering when they stamp on an ant-hill, can you answer me that? No-one. I talk to them sometimes, to keep them company when I have nothing better to do, but they're tiresome . . . They want me to put myself in their position though none of them ever once thinks of putting himself in mine. I want to bring them some comfort, but all they can do is complain. Some of them still have telephones. They try to get in touch with those close to them or the emergency services, but they use up all their credit or their batteries in the maze of automatic switchboards that will never be able to connect them to the person they want to contact. And anyway, what would they be able to do? What can we do for them? Nothing, I've already told you. After all, I'm not the one who's put them where they are. And if this was indeed placed within the realm of my responsibility, it was such a long time ago that there must be a statute of limitations now."

There was a silence, for a fraction of a second, or a thousand years, who could say? Time had become an incidental dimension. The Investigator's body was visibly melting. He was coming apart, cooked by the sun, twisted and squeezed like a floorcloth being wrung out one last time before it's thrown into the rubbish.

"Most fortunately," the Shadow went on, "these poor creatures don't last very long. To begin with, they howl like pigs getting their throats cut, and then very quickly they weaken, and then end up going quiet. For evermore. The great silence. Why would you want to take it out on me? What a funny idea! What can I do about it? As if it were anything to do with me! To each his destiny. You think it's easy to sweep here? Everyone gets what he deserves. There are no innocents. Don't you think?"

"I don't know . . . I don't know anymore . . ." the Investigator said. "Where are we? In Hell?"

The Shadow almost choked and gave a big laugh that ended in a horrible coughing fit. He hawked and spat into the distance three times over.

"In Hell! That really is going a bit far! You do like simplistic explanations, don't you? I don't think such things apply nowadays. The world is too complex. The old tricks no longer work. And anyway, men are no longer children to whom we can still tell this kind of nonsense. No, you're plainly here in a sort of transit area of The Firm, which has been transformed over time into a big open-air dump. This is where they cram whatever can't be put anywhere else, whatever is out of service, things, objects, rotting stuff, anything no-one knows what to do with. I could show you whole hills covered in prostheses, wooden legs, soiled bandages, pharmaceutical waste, valleys weighed down with the corpses of mobile telephones, computers, printed circuit boards, silicon, lakes filled to the brim with fluorocarbon, toxic mud and acid mud, geological faults plugged up with large shovelfuls of radioactive material, tar sands, not to mention the rivers carrying millions of hectolitres of engine lubrication oil, chemical fertiliser, solvents, pesticides, forests whose trees are constructions made of rusty scrap-iron girders, metallic structures adorned with reinforced concrete, molten plastic combined with thousands of tons of used syringes that end up looking like branches stripped of their leaves, and I don't know what else. What do you want me to do, I can't clean everything up for them, all I've got is this!"

The Shadow punctuated his words with waves of the broom.

"This place is nothing yet," he went on. "It's a new territory. A landscape in progress, waiting for the artists who some day will celebrate it, and the walkers who will come, sooner or later, with their families on Sundays for a picnic. We're just beginning. For now I've only seen containers arriving, prefabs built in haste according to need. The Firm is developing so fast. You have to wonder who is in charge, as I don't understand its strategy. It needs new sites, but it also gets rid of them just as quickly, as it's simultaneously in a perpetual state of restructuring, and there can sometimes be regrettable mistakes of which some people are victims. The rates of production they're forced to meet are such that the Transporters load the containers even while there are still men working in them. Unlucky for them, but all they had to do was get out in time. You pay dearly for lapses in concentration or over-zealousness nowadays. Overtime digs the graves of those who accumulate it. The age of the utopians has passed. It'll always be possible to buy dreams, sometime later, on credit, from antique dealers, in private collections or second-hand village markets, but to what end? To show them to children? Will there still be any children? Do you have children? Have you reproduced? Man is a negligible quantity nowadays, a minor species with a special talent for disaster. He's now nothing more than a risk to be run."

The Shadow expelled another thick glob of sticky, greenish spittle, which fell to the dust and traced out a slender-bodied snake with an oblong head which sank into the earth without a moment's pause.

"And so according to you," he went on, looking at the Investigator through his blindfold, "what is it I'm meant to have founded?"

# 42

THE INVESTIGATOR REALLY FELT AS THOUGH HE WERE JUST ABOUT
to vanish once and for all. Perhaps he already had done? His
existence was now only written intermittently, like a dotted line, or
a flickering neon bulb, giving off a noise resembling that made by
fragile summer-evening insects when they come right up close to
street lamps and burn there. Now he only lived by fits and starts, in
brief accesses of consciousness that left gaps of blackness between
them, thick wells of tar, at the heart of which there was nothing
happening, nothing he could remember.

And it was not hunger, or thirst, or tiredness that was the cause
of all this. It was not even the continuous obstacles scattered in
his path. Deep down, what was eating away at him, in this final
protected part of his soul that still produced some measure of feeling, behind the last ramparts that were still holding out, while the
great defensive walls, the look-out posts, the moats, the draw-
bridges, the watchtowers, everything, had been destroyed in a
progressive collapse, a process of sabotage that had been underway
since his arrival in the Town, was the disappointment at discovering
that he had been a useless worker and that he never would have

had the strength to achieve the goal that had been assigned to him: to understand why men had surrendered themselves to death, that is, why men at a certain moment in their existence had decided to refuse the game of Humanity, no longer to await the irreversible degeneration of their organism, the ruptured aneurysm, the proliferation of metastases, the obstruction from an accumulation of fat in one of their main arteries, an accident on the road or at home, murder, drowning, bacteriological warfare, a bombing, an earthquake, a tidal wave, a major flood, to meet death. Why men – five of them, or ten, two dozen or thousands, the exact number hardly mattered – had gone against their deepest instinct that ordered them to survive at all costs, to keep up the struggle, to accept the unacceptable because the religion of life should be stronger than the despair engendered by the piling up of obstacles? Why men – at the heart of The Firm or elsewhere, that was quite incidental – had given up their overalls, their badges, their uniforms of mankind? How could he, this simple Investigator, this poor wretch, have understood this and explained it?

Malfunction was becoming his essence. In the grip of an irreversible short-circuit, the Investigator struggled in a confusion of seconds which created in his exhausted mind a collage of moments he had lived through, of deliria, of dreams, of fantasies, of things remembered and anticipated, and the bombardment of images to which he was subjected, from which he couldn't escape, ended up breaking apart his consciousness, fragmenting it like a grenade touching the ground and scattering its various fragments in a rainbow of death.

"You haven't answered my question. Is that normal for you?" the Founder persisted.

"What question?" murmured the Investigator, who had just got back to his feet, in a very provisional way, for the final scene of his life, in which the motionless sun was spreading a heat that was get-ting harder and harder to bear. "Someone is toying with me, aren't they . . . ? I'm not measuring up to my own life. This sun . . . Isn't it just a lamp behind a thick magnifying glass above my head . . . ? Am I still being watched? Tell me. Is this still the experiment? Have I passed the earlier tests? Please, tell me . . . Will I be able to investigate?"

"You're answering my question with questions, a rather facile strategy, don't you think?"

The Shadow's voice sounded irritated.

"For I don't know how long we've been here together, I've been putting up with you, and now I'm waiting for your answer. What do you think? You think I know more than you? Sometimes you tinker with things, you try to invent things, and everything just blows up in your face. You want to stop the bleeding, but there's no way! So what to do? Fret about it? No, personally I've just decided to turn my back on it. Cowardice isn't the failing people think it is. Courage often does more damage. Let them cope on their own!"

The Investigator no longer understood a thing the Shadow was saying. He couldn't feel his feet on the ground. He felt as though his body were floating in the air, as though he were no longer really touching the earth. His arms had taken on the insubstantiality of fog. There was nothing left of his hands, dense as incense smoke, but the palms, volatile, ashen, through which the light was already passing, revealed thousands of particles spun about by conflicting currents, and majestic tremors that ended up carrying them off in waves, in whirlpools, in spirals, dashing them down into wells where they became stars in the middle of darkness, combining afterwards into an infinity of Milky Ways in the depths of which it was possible to make out mauve flashes of explosions, universal cataclysms, the deafening collisions of asteroids, of comets, and of bodies hurled since the dawn of time into the purest void.

"Don't worry about anything anymore," the Shadow went on, "don't trouble yourself about yourself any longer. Your fingers won't come back. Nor will the rest. It will all be eaten away, bit by bit, there's nothing you can do about it, and anyway, it's painless. I guarantee you that. Rather try to answer my question, you can still do that if you want to. Make the most of this extraordinary luck you've had in escaping from the container, try and give it some meaning, answer my question: what is it, according to you, that I've founded?"

The Shadow's voice circled around the Investigator, entered him, flowed into what was left of his chest, filled his whole skull. The heat was more and more dreadful, and when he tried to mop his forehead with the back of one of his hands he found that he no longer had hands, and that his forehead, too, had disappeared.

"I'm going . . ." he managed to whisper, fearful, surprised and disappointed.

"Clearly!" the Shadow taunted him. "Why are you surprised? And yet dying should not surprise he who is nobody, the Poet once wrote. But no-one reads poetry anymore. Men wipe their arses with it! What's more, I did notify you that you were going to disappear soon, I didn't deceive you, I never lie, I'm not like that. Come on, damn it, make the most of your last moments, give some meaning to your agony if you haven't known how to give meaning to your life: answer me, you have nothing to lose now. What have I founded? Tell me, dammit! Do you want me to get down on my knees? Apparently that has worked in the past."

And then, not knowing why, the Investigator dreamed of lilacs and their scent. He clearly saw the blossoms in mauve bunches sagging in a distant spring of a May morning, and he breathed in their potent, sweet smell. Then he was on a ship, more precisely at its prow, which was going at more than thirty knots, his two hands holding the rail as the sea spray streamed across his face and left the delicious taste of water and salt on his lips, and the foamy waves gushed with schools of dolphins, caressed by the songs of sirens that welled up in the air that dazzled with light. He also saw a child coming out of its mother's belly, thighs torn apart groaning out the little body delivered in a joyful effort and the mother's tears mingling with the blood and the stuff of life being born. Then he was right in the middle of a dancing crowd celebrating the restoration of peace after a war that had claimed millions of victims. He was spun around, he was entwined by women who placed their hot lips on his, he saw their laughter, their eyes that shone with joy, and he caressed their hips and their breasts, forgot himself in them and then suddenly there was nothing.

"One could go on, with other images, if I were to allow you," said the Shadow, who sounded rather put out. "It's easy to believe in happiness. All it takes is grafting a few moments like those into one or two cells in your brain and it's done. I'm going to offer you the treat of enjoying these final little pleasures that you have never known, these tuppenny-ha'penny false memories, to prove to you that I'm not a bad fellow, but now answer me! I want to hear it from a man's mouth: what is it I'm supposed to have founded?"

Where had that great incandescent sun got to? And that vast plain with the chalk ground? Was it night time, at last? the Investigator wondered, unable to make out anything any longer, and he realised, helpless, that his final, feeble powers were deserting him.

"Not yet," the Shadow whispered, "not yet, that would be too simple . . . The night, that is for later."

Yet it had all begun so normally. In a station that resembled many other stations. On a square such as the Earth had in limitless numbers. In the most ordinary sort of bar. Why, then, did everything get complicated? He had set foot in a new town, or in a new life. He had come across characters, people who counted for millions of others. He had attempted to arrange the cards, to give names, to simplify, to clarify, to go where he had been told to go, to do what he had been told to do. Even the narrative of events had, to begin with, followed familiar codes, playing itself out on reassuring architectures before it began to free itself from them, to come loose, to saw off the branches on which it had sat for so long, helping to disorient him still further.

"I had an Investigation to conduct," the Investigator said softly, trying in vain to touch his chin to his chest which no longer existed. "An Investigation I wasn't even able to start . . ."

"What do you know? Who says you didn't carry out this Investigation successfully, since you found me, since – according to you – I am the Founder?"

"I wasn't looking for you, I had an Investigation . . ." muttered the Investigator before his lips dissolved and his face with them.

"*It is by not seeking that you find.* Am I perhaps the reason for all this as well as its consequence? The beginning and the end of the cycle? What do you know about it? You call me the Founder, but who knows, I might be the Gravedigger, too, mightn't I? That would suit me better! Remember all these containers! I'm surrounded by corpses. Come on, then, hurry up and answer my question, you won't last for ever. You maintained that you were the Investigator. You had a mission, a function, a goal, and even if you don't think you reached your objective the fact remains that you always know who you are, and why that's what you are, but as for me, what am I, really? I've had a broom put into my hands, I don't know when, but that doesn't make much sense. What is my function here? WHAT AM I THE FOUNDER OF?" yelled the Shadow, and his shout rebounded in a cascade of echoes that dissolved in an extended fall, bruising one another, making the ground and the sky tremble in an alarum of thunder.

The Shadow waited, but the Investigator turned away from him as he saw ghosts come to greet him, as in a ritual of condolences, silhouettes, ideas, reminiscences, holograms, fictional characters among whom he clearly recognised the Policeman, the Giantess – who smiled at him – the Guide, the Manager, the Waiter, the Sentry and the Guard, the Child with the burning eyes, the Psychologist set back a little, the Tourists, The Displaced, the Crowd. All of them seemed a little embarrassed. They were gathering before the body of a man, of medium build, round face, bald head, who resembled them like a brother, a man who was the victim of a farce in which they had played their part, without trying too hard to get out of it, because it's much less trouble that way. They had always been some distance ahead of the Investigator, and they still were now, even if it was of no use to them and would not save them.

There were letters, too, assembled by a hand that drew them on a blackboard. A needle piercing a vein to draw blood from it, or to inject some liquid, the very pure image of a medical drip and its soothing music, the sound soon overlaid by the rustle of sheets of paper being torn up for burning and the whisper of ink that flows onto the page of a book.

"SO WHAT HAVE I FOUNDED!!!???" the Shadow screamed one last time.

In the Investigator's weak, lost soul, one or two silent words still trembled, just barely sketched out, before what was left of his consciousness was carried off into the void, like the final puff of a cigarette taken by the wind. Then everything in him died, the answer to the question, the signs, the traces of light, memory, doubt. He thought he heard a faint sound, like the sound made by the screen of a laptop being closed onto its keyboard still warm from the fingers that have brushed over it for so long.

*Clack.*

And then nothing more.

Nothing more.

PHILIPPE CLAUDEL is a novelist, film director and university lecturer. His film "I've Loved You So Long" won the 2008 BAFTA for Best Film Not In English. His novel *Brodeck's Report* was winner of the 2010 *Independent* Foreign Fiction Prize.

DANIEL HAHN is a writer, editor and translator from Spanish, Portuguese and French. His translations include *The Book of Chameleons* by José Eduardo Agualusa, which won the 2007 *Independent* Foreign Fiction Prize.